Copyright © 2013 Waheeda Soomro

All rights reserved. Except as permitted under the U.S. Copyright Act 1976, no part of this publication may be reproduced, distributed or transmitted in any form without the prior, written permission of the author.

The characters and events portrayed in this story are fictitious. Any similarity to real persons, living or dead, business establishments or locales is coincidental and not intended by the author. In the event a real name is used, it is used fictitiously.

The cover illustrations have been graciously contributed by artist – Sayeeda Khan.

ISBN-13: 978-1482683059
ISBN-10: 1482683059

Love one another,
but make not a bond of love:
Let it rather be a moving sea between
the shores of your souls.

by Khalil Gibran

UNSPOKEN

Waheeda Soomro

Dedication

I would like to dedicate this book to my mother Aliya Khatoon, and to all mothers whose lives are so easily left UNSPOKEN.

I was the last of her nine children; she died at an early age of 45; fighting a tough war with breast cancer. I was around 16 when she passed away. These are some of the meager facts of her life that I know.

I knew her as my mother, as my father's wife and as a loving aunt and sister to all of her relatives. Throughout those sixteen years, I only saw her giving to others. She had to face many difficulties in her life, and this made her very strong; she would always stand up for what was right and just.

I admire my mother, and love her immensely, but I never knew her as Aliya. How did she grow up? Did she have a good childhood, who were her friends, did any mishaps happen in her life? What were her fears, her sorrows and her joys? Today when I go and stand at my mother's grave, I feel ashamed that I never tried to learn more about her. I was just concerned that she should be a good mother to me. She knew much about my life, and that I was a part of her, yet very little do I know about her.

I am an emotional fool. I don't want to remember all those times when she yelled at me, or ignored me; I only want to remember those few moments when she hugged me or caressed me. For me she was my mother and that is all that my heart wants to recall.

Each one of us carries a story within us, and this story is not ordinary, it is unique and special because it is the story of a human being.

My heart had been so restless over these years; it has been nearly 18 years since my mother passed away. I could never come to terms with this lack of compassion on my part; of not being able to know my mother.

I would wonder and make stories of how I thought my mother went through her life. But I can never compensate for the void that this lack of knowledge has left in my soul.

This book is an apology and a dedication, not only to my mother, but to every woman. We are not mere shadows that pass through the night, but we are god's creations and we share this universe with each other. Shouldn't we at least try to know each other?

One of the greatest women to have shared this world with us was Mother Teresa, and in her words I conclude:

"*We may not do a lot of great things in life, but we can do a lot of small things with great love.*"

Introduction

This story is a realistic fiction. The names of characters and locations seem real but they do not in any way represent any event or person, living or dead.

I am just a storyteller; hence please forgive me if I have not spent my vision on describing the details of the characters or their surroundings.

I have always invested my creativity in trying to put this in words: the feelings, the pain, and the suffering that young girls and women have to endure silently.

The setting is fictitious, but the problems and sufferings spelt out in this tale are very real and dire.

This is not the story of one or a few people; it is the story of millions of women, living in this day and century.

I hope you don't invest your attention in trying to find faults or loop holes, but seek instead to sear your heart with the pain and lamenting of a million silent hearts like you and I.

This plot is not romantic or historical, but it is a

piece of reality that could not be left *unspoken*.

Part I
SHARMEEN

1

The flight was to arrive at 8:30 pm, and that was rush hour going to Heathrow Airport. My fingers drummed the steering wheel, enjoying a Sufi ghazal sung by Nusrat Fateh Ali Khan. I met my eyes in the rear view mirror – they looked so happy. She was coming home, my darling daughter Nadia. She had gone to Egypt for four years to study Archeology.

Somehow, just like sadness, happiness was all too readable on my face. My cheeks felt warm, trying to hold back a gleaming smile. I exhaled and accepted the bliss of the moment. As I turned onto Bath Road, my heart pounded faster. I hated the airport's covered parking; it always made me feel caged.

I ran up the escalator; peering over my shoulder at the information board, I saw her plane had arrived. I thought she might be in customs by now, I hoped I wasn't late. Airports are a place of self-restraint, you learn to hold on and hug, and let go and say goodbyes. You see smiles and tears all at the same time, same place.

The sun was setting and I could see only half of the 747, glaring in the light. As I looked away, I could see a group of people hustling and bustling around something. Trying to get a closer look, I moved in a little. A small gap in the group of people revealed a glimpse of a man lying on the ground.

A while later the paramedics arrived, and as they opened up the tight circle of people, I saw that it was an elderly man lying sideways on the floor. Somebody whispered, "It's a cardiac." I heard the elderly man say something to the medic; his voice, though very faint, sent fearful chills down my spine. I could recognize that voice even after twenty-five years, and in a crowd of millions. I pushed the crowd around and went in for a better look, the man looked very old and withered, very different from how my mind had engraved him in my memory. It had been twenty-five years since I had last seen him. But I was sure that it was Yusuf, even though age had distorted his handsome face, and the words that had once churned many a heart were now so feeble and faint. I was numb. I had waited for this moment all my life, to be able to have one last glimpse of Yusuf. I had feared this moment too, for I wasn't sure if his reappearance would shatter me again. I kept standing there, frozen in the moment, staring at my first love. For one second Yusuf saw me standing very close to him. His stare was blank, and this man for whom I had drained my heart did not even remember me. A frenzy of emotions engulfed me, I wanted to go to him, and introduce myself to him. I wanted to tell him how I had wasted my entire life thinking that he loved me. I felt as enraged and ashamed at this thought; I had broken my father's trust for this callous and self-centered man. My father would never have forgiven me, and I would have had to carry the shattered fragments of his faith, like spears in my heart.

Yusuf looked at me again, our eyes met, and then without any emotion, he turned his face away. He definitely had not recognized me; I was just a stranger to him. After all, it had been twenty-five years. He had forgotten me. Apparently he had never loved me. I was just a fleeting moment in his life. Yusuf Ali was once again making me fall apart, and I hated myself for this weakness. I wished that my Baba was near me, to hold me, and take me away from this man.

I felt faint, but right then, someone hugged me

from behind, "Mom, I'm here." Seeing Nadia, my mind flashed back to the present, and once again I forgot everything and I smiled. Nadia held my hand and my hand was ice cold, she looked worried and inquired if I was feeling well. Nadia sat me down, and got me cold lemonade from the airport café…The sugar in the drink nourished my weakened nerves and I rationalized aloud that since I had not eaten for a while, the lack of food was making me feel faint. Nadia lovingly rubbed my back and said, "You know you need to take care of yourself, Mom." She kissed my cheek and helped me get up and walk to the car. I turned around to see an ambulance taking Yusuf away from me, but what my mind was seeing was an ocean of tears that lay between us.

Nadia offered to drive back, but I didn't want her driving on these busy city streets. On the ride back home, it was hard for me to concentrate on the road, as on one side Nadia kept chatting and on the other side Yusuf's helpless face kept bringing tears to my eyes. I had not expected to see him in that condition.

We reached home and I got busy setting dinner for both of us; yes, it was only two of us now, as my husband, Abbas Bakhtiar, had passed away about seven years ago fighting with pancreatic cancer.

Unspoken

During dinner, Nadia continued her nonstop chattering, telling me about her experiences in Egypt. I tried very hard to stare intensely at her face, so that no other face would sear into my eyes. A bit of her conversation alerted me, she started to talk about that man in the airport, who had suffered a heart attack. She said that she had been told by a person there that he was a poet from India, attending a poetic function here. I asked her if she knew which hospital they had taken him to. "Hilling-don Hospital, I guess," she said, "that's the closest to the airport." Nadia kept chatting as I distracted my mind by finishing my chores, and then we sat and had her favorite ice cream. She started unpacking her stuff. She showed me her pictures on the laptop. One snapshot interested me – it was an old Egyptian temple, made of red mud, and everything around it was also red. She said it was the lost city, and it has been standing there for centuries. Now archaeologists were digging up the past through it.

I don't know why, but I felt a kind of affinity towards that monument that stood there for centuries, witnessing and holding so much unspoken truth. I told her that sometimes the past should be left silent in the sands of time.

She smiled. "You know, Mom, I love to learn about the past, that's why I took Archeology." I smiled and tucked her in bed and said, "Okay, my little Indy, time to sleep."

She reminded me that her fiancé Ahmed and his family would be arriving tomorrow evening for the wedding preparations, and that the wedding was scheduled for two weeks later. I told her I remembered – "I'm not *that* old," I said – and that tomorrow morning I would show her all the wedding shopping I had done for her from India.

I sat down on my bed. The room was very dark, and I turned on my bedside lamp. The light turned on dim, and as it became brighter and brighter my tears began to twinkle in my eyes and I realized I was crying. The pain that I had held in my heart for so many years had suddenly become so visible to me. I reached for the notebook in my bedside drawer. My life story, which I had started writing recently in Lucknow; I had reached my present trudging through my past. Then why was my past again staring at me through Yusuf's eyes? I had confronted my weakness, and my pain; word by word, the truth lay scribbled through those pages of my notebook. Why now, did my past find me again, why?

Unspoken

I dimmed the light, and lay quietly in darkness. Curled up tightly in my bed, I was yearning for someone to hold me, I was falling apart. I couldn't sleep, so I picked up my notebook, turned on the light on dim and let my mind drift through the pages of my past.

2

I begin from where my memory serves me. I was around ten years old when we moved to Lucknow from Kanpur. My father, whom I lovingly called "Baba," was an advocate for the high court in Kanpur. Lucknow and Kanpur city are located in India close to each other. From the very beginning I loved Lucknow.

Lucknow is famous for its rich culture and traditional living. Basically, the tradition there was to enjoy life, have kebobs, and listen to Urdu poetry. It was often called the "Princely state," that is, the city of Nawabs or royalty. It was said that half of the people living in Lucknow were poets, and poets of different levels. No other career charmed them. And due to this heavy competition, most poets were willing to read at street corners and were always handsomely praised and rewarded by the crowds. They kept the soul of Lucknow alive. Attending such street-side poetry contests with my father from the age of ten, I began to develop a taste for writing and a philosophical mind.

In Kanpur the court house was a big commute for my father, so he hardly got to spend any time with me. Here in Lucknow the court was two miles away. Baba would come home early, and wasn't that tired. Every evening I would wait near my window, looking out for the horse carriage, or tanga, that my father used for transportation. Mom and I would stay all dressed up since Baba would take us out to the Aminabad market for treats and to enjoy the hustle-bustle of the city market. Sometimes we would sit on benches on the street corner and have the famous *tunde kebobs*. Even today my lungs are filled with that aroma. It is said that the person who first started making these kebobs on the streets of Lucknow was one-handed. In the Urdu language such a person is called *tunda*, and thus the name became tunde kebobs. This was in the 1950s, and to this day these kebobs are still the most famous thing in Lucknow. It is amazing; no one knows the real name of that man, but the recipe has been passed over from generation to generation. The kebobs are made of ground goat meat or beef and are marinated overnight in about a hundred and sixty different spices. The women of the family had been appointed to perform this daily ritual. Next evening the kebobs would be roasted on an open charcoal grill. The result is heavenly; you eat them with bread called naan. Mom loved the street food, and would always ask Baba to pack some extras for the next day's lunch.

By the time we were ready for Baba to hail a tanga so we could go home, I would be hazy with sleep. In the tanga, lying down on my father's lap, I loved to see the bright, colorful lights that decorated the market streets. My father would close my eyes with his loving hand and pat me to sleep. I would give out a deep sigh, settle down comfortably in his lap and sink into sleep. The day had now ended for me, my Baba was home and he was with me. This was my most cherished moment, because this was the only moment in which I could be in my father's arms, and I felt that he loved me.

3

SELMA

The first few years of school in Lucknow were really lonely. I was very shy and didn't make friends easily. I met Selma in grade seven when she had moved here from Bhopal. It was her first day that year. She sat in the chair next to mine. We liked each other at once. She needed a friend, and I was waiting for one. Selma had moved two streets away from my house. We began to share a tanga to school and back. Though it was only about an eight-minute ride to her house, and ten minutes to mine, we cherished that time.

In Lucknow, some people still used horse-driven tangas, just to keep the culture alive, and Baba hired a tanga driver called Baban. Baba had bought the tanga from a moneylender, who was selling it quite cheap. Baba didn't want me to travel by public transport, as he didn't think it was safe for girls. Baban was a very simple and humble person; Baba liked him.

He came from a very poor family, and was the only member earning money. He had a daughter named Raffia who was thirteen, and a son named Jabbar who was ten. I loved talking to Baban on our way to school. I had gathered from his talks that he was always worried about saving money for his daughter's dowry.

Sometimes, Mom would ask Baban to drop Raffia at our house in the morning, so that she could help with the housecleaning and other chores. This was Mom's way of helping out Baban, to make a little more money for Raffia's dowry. Mom knew that it was difficult to take care of a daughter, especially if one was poor. Mom had told me that Raffia was engaged to a man who was about fifteen years older than her, and this man kept twisting Baban's hands with more demands for the dowry.

Baba would yell at Baban for indulging in this man's greed, but Mom knew that Baban didn't have a choice; a father's hardest job was to get his daughter married. Raffia wasn't very good looking, and she was dark in complexion, which made it more difficult to get a groom for her.

Raffia studied till grade six, and then she had to leave school, as her parents thought it was more important to get her married soon.

Ours was an all-girls convent school, one of the best in Lucknow. It was run by British nuns. We had a very strict uniform code: white long-sleeved shirt, and grey pinafore with white full-length slacks. Lucknow being a very conservative place, girls were required to keep their legs covered. We were not allowed to wear dresses or skirts. Some of the girls came from very conservative families and were supposed to wear a scarf on their heads, and some even wore a black *burkha* from head to toe. It covered even their faces. Luckily, my family and Selma's weren't that strict.

Mom and Baba were very particular about our culture. Girls must speak softly, no giggling around, as it attracted undue attention. We had to learn to cook at a young age and do the household chores. We were religious, but not very strict Muslims. I being the only child, Mom was very indulgent with me, and I always escaped my chores. Mom really spoiled me a lot. Every day when I got back from school, she would have some snack ready for me in the kitchen. She knew I liked spicy food, like her, so we normally had samosas or pakoras with cold mint chatni.

After I had taken a shower, Mom would sit down

with me, to help me with my homework or to just inquire how my day went. Most of the time I would do my homework on the breakfast table in our kitchen, where Mom would be busy cooking fresh dinner for us.

Raffia had become a constant part of our kitchen. Mom would lovingly teach her how to cook, and would speak loudly, for her instructions were meant for me, too. No matter how busy Mom was with her chores, she always knew what Baba and I needed, and she provided it at the right time. We could totally depend on her. After dinner, Raffia would leave with leftovers; Mom saw to it that she had enough food for her entire family. Mom would also pay her generously for her help.

Selma had one brother, and her mother had died in childbirth. Selma and her brother needed someone to take care of them, so her father was forced to remarry to a woman named Safia, who did not have any children of her own. They had moved to Lucknow, because Selma's dad, Imtiaz, got a better position in the courthouse, and the salary was better. Selma's stepmother would always harass her husband that he wasn't making enough money. She was from a well-to-do family, but since she had a defect in one of her legs, her parents took the first offer that came for her. Her family was in Hyderabad; that is why, when they had to move to Lucknow, Safia wasn't happy. Her husband, Imtiaz, was just an office clerk at the courthouse. That wasn't a prestigious position for her. Her own father was an advocate for the Supreme Court.

Selma was quite a pretty little thing. She was very dainty, about five feet, very fair skinned, big gorgeous eyes, and deep pink lips. I would tell Selma that she looked like a Kashmir doll. She was so fair that when she drank a cola, I could actually see it pass through her throat.

The only thing I didn't like about Selma was that while she had such swaying long hair right down to her hips, she would always drench it in jasmine oil. I would tease her by saying, "You have so much oil in your hair that we can fry the pakoras in it." She looked so beautiful when she didn't oil her hair. She braided her hair tightly, and put in little hair ties that had small bells attached to them. I hated putting oil in my hair. Mom would force me to apply oil every Sunday, and it was like torture time. Mom would always point out how Selma was such a good girl, she never complained about the oil. Mom didn't know, but everyone else in school complained about the strong, sweet smell that the oil gave out.

Sometimes, I would catch Selma's braid and walk behind her, singing, "Jingle bell, jingle bell…" She was full of life, loud, boisterous, funny but courageous, and a very affectionate and compassionate girl. From the very beginning I was in awe of her. She had so much bitterness and lack in her life, but that did not stop her from enjoying the life that God had given her. She made me want to live and be happy too. She completed me.

In our culture, men were given priority over women. Mom never ate till Baba came home, no matter how late it was. She wore the clothes that he chose for her – not that he inhibited her tastes in any way. If she liked something, he would encourage her to get it. My father remained not just a husband but my mother's admirer till she died. He liked everything about her. He would praise her looks, the food she cooked, and the way she spoke and took care of the house.

My father married late due to his studies, and my mom was fifteen years younger than him. There were two things that my dad liked best on her: her dainty little silver anklets that had little bells in them

Unspoken

and chimed as she walked around the house, and the champa flowers that she wore in her hair every evening. Their fragrance could make my dad forget the whole world. That's what he used to tell her.

4

My mom's name was Yasmeen and my dad's name was Shoaib Kazi, or should I say Advocate Shoaib Kazi. I was named Sharmeen Kazi, by my beloved uncle or Mamu. Mamu was my mom's elder brother. Even when we were in Kanpur, Mamu visited us often; his main reason for the visit would always be me. I was his little doll. Mamu didn't have any children, and he loved children. Mamu had a very round and chubby face, dotted with marks of smallpox. I would love to hang around his neck and pull his cheeks. Mamu never minded anything I did. He was quite short; I think just about five feet, so I always treated him as my equal, a kid. He loved being a child with me, or any other kid. Even at the early age of forty, Mamu had lost most of his hair; he tried every traditional remedy under the sun, but no hair grew.

I remember from the time that I could remember, Mamu would take me out, buy me whatever I wanted, and tell me lovely bedtime stories. In all his stories, I was the pretty princess. That is why when we had to move to Lucknow, I was especially pleased. We would be living right next to Mamu's house!

We were all very proud of my father. He would take up a lot of cases for the poor and would not take any fees in return. All his friends thought he was a fool – a lawyer who did not take any money? This was the weirdest thing. During one such suit, my father met Yusuf Ali. Yusuf was very much like my father. He was his junior, about seven years younger than him. Yusuf didn't care about money; he loved to fight for justice, and loved poetry. He was himself a very good poet.

School had become very pleasant since Selma had enrolled in it. During lunch break Selma and I would often sit under the banyan tree at the corner of our school playground. We would enjoy the cool winter breeze, from the swaying long branches of the banyan tree. It would lull us and take away all our troubles. Not that we had too many troubles then, except our mean math teacher. We dreaded him and we hated math.

The lunch that we most liked was a bag of potato chips, bread and ketchup. Selma would spread some ketchup on the bread and crunch some chips on the two slices. Trust me, it was a heavenly crunch for us; the best fast food in those times.

Selma's stepmother always found faults in her, and Selma became the cause of fights between her stepmother and her father. After school, Selma would get off at my place and spend some time at our house before going back to her hurting world. Mom would be taking her afternoon nap at that time. We would rush into the house and wake her up. Years later, I discovered that Mom was actually awake, anxiously waiting for me, but she pretended to be asleep.

I remember mom telling Aunt Jamila our neighbor, "How can a mother of a young girl take afternoon naps, who hardly sleeps even at night? I want to be with my daughter as much as I can. I do not know how much time I have left to be with her."

That was Mom's blackmailing statement – one day soon I'll die, and then you'll miss me.

And my dad would joke around and say, "No dear, you can't die so soon. Who will buy the champa flowers, and have arguments with the meat man every day, and who would feed the birds and the squirrels? They would all die without you." My mom would make those big eyes and stare at us and say, "Yes, everyone will miss me except you two." Mom didn't know that life would very soon play a very unkind joke on her.

For me, Mom was the most beautiful woman I had ever seen. Every time she hugged me, her fragrance would soothe every corner of my soul. She was about five feet four inches in height, wheat-like complexion, eyes shaped like almonds. Long silky hair, that ran straight below her hips. Her feet were very dainty, and the little anklets that she wore on them made one want to just gaze at her pretty feet. She had a perfect figure, was very soft spoken and spoke very eloquent Urdu. I would stare at her for hours as she dressed. I wished that one day I would be as pretty as her. She always wore cotton *sarees* with pastel floral prints. On her waist she hung a silver key chain, with tiny bells attached to it. We always knew if Mom was passing by – the little tiny bells chimed softly. It felt as if a gentle breeze had just teased a million wind chimes. Baba loved that.

5

One night, without any warning, it began to pour. Mom woke up to lightning and thunder.

She woke up Dad and said, "I need to go to the terrace. I just put the clothes to dry this evening, I need to bring the clothes down." Dad was too sleepy to get up, so she came and woke me up. She shouted, "Just get up now!" I dragged my sleepy feet to the stairway. Mom ran up the stairs, opened the terrace door, and began gathering the clothes. I could feel the gust of the moist wind as she opened the terrace door, it was really pouring. I trudged up the stairs, and saw Mom getting wet in the rain. "Mom," I said, "I'm not coming out there in the rain; please bring the clothes to me and I'll take them down." She gathered an armful of clothes and gave them to me. The clothes were dripping by now. I walked down slowly, on the now cold and wet stone stairway. I walked to the bathroom and dumped the clothes into the bathtub. That is when I heard the scariest thud.

I ran from the bathroom, but my heart raced faster. My fear had come true. Mom had slipped on the wet steps and was lying on the bottom of the stairway. She lay absolutely still. There was blood surrounding her head, and the pool of blood kept getting bigger. I clung against the wall; my nails dug deep, and with all my strength, I screamed, "Baba!" Baba was instantly there.

That was the first time in my life that I had seen Baba cry like a child. He was numb, scared and very confused. He touched Mom's head and kept calling out to her. The blood was now oozing from her mouth. I suddenly gained a sense of urgency and I ran to call for an ambulance. I shook Dad and said that we had to take Mom to a hospital. He sat there, regressed to a ten-year-old child, not able to move a muscle. He just kept repeating, "But why, why?"

Mom had left us long before we reached the hospital. I called Mamu, since I was too young to sign any hospital papers and Baba was not himself. Everything that I knew, felt and understood about life had suddenly changed in few short hours. My mother had left me alone in this world. My father was more like a child now. I wanted to scream.

I wanted to fall apart. But I knew I had no one to hold me.

It rained a lot that night as we drove back from the hospital. When I entered our home, it was so still and silent, as if there was no more life in it. There was a stench of blood all around. I slowly walked towards the stairway; reality lay spilled in the form of my mother's blood. It took me a while to actually find the awareness that the blood had to be cleaned. Selma saw us coming back from the hospital. Mamu had informed them about Mom's death. Selma came in and saw me staring at the blood as though hypnotized. She came close to me, held my hand and said, "You go to your room, I will clean this." I willingly walked away; I knew it was too horrific for me to smear my hands with my mother's blood. Baba dragged his feet, fell flopped on Mom's side of the bed and cried like a baby. I could not sleep. I stayed up, watching the storm outside, trying to calm the storm within me.

A few days after the funeral, I began cleaning up the house and taking up Mom's chores. Going to school and managing house was a bit tough, but I was not left with any choices.

Even though Mom was not there, the house still had to run the way it used to. Raffia would come and help me out with the cooking and cleaning. It was tough, because Mom had done everything for me. All I knew was some basic cooking, which Mom had forcefully made me watch and learn. I used to watch Mom doing her chores. Every night before Mom went to bed she would iron my clothes for school and Baba's clothes for his work. Baba's suit had to be ironed and his shirt starched every night. Mom would make homemade starch from rice starch and water. She would then sprinkle the starch on Baba's shirt, and iron it very firmly with a heavy iron, so that the wrinkles would fade away.

I never realized how intense of a chore this was, till I finally had to do it.

Along with his suit, Baba needed a white handkerchief. This also had to be ironed and folded neatly. After that, perfumed oil, made from a fragrant grass called *khas*, would be very lightly smeared in the center of the kerchief. The suit was now ready and would be hung on an old-fashioned wooden hanger, and the kerchief placed on Baba's dresser. Every bit of Baba's grooming was done by Mom with great love. She enjoyed pampering him and me.

In the morning I would polish Baba's shoes and place them near his suit, with matching socks. Once Baba was ready, he would take the handkerchief and gently pat it on his forehead and on the back of his neck. Khas is supposed to have cooling and anti-stress properties. The kerchief would be carefully placed in his front coat pocket. The fold on the kerchief had to be precise, so that it fit perfectly into the coat pocket without getting ruffled.

While Baba got dressed, I myself would get dressed for school, and make breakfast for the two of us. Baba ate one boiled egg and two pieces of toast, with a cup of chai or black tea, with milk and sugar. I, on the other hand, ate anything that I could grab while running out for school. It was very strange that I had slipped into Mom's role so easily, as that's what was unquestionably expected of me.

Sometimes on Sunday mornings, I would call the street vendor that sold fresh milk cream or *malai*, and Baba would bring in some hot *jalebees*. This would be our Sunday brunch. Selma would often join us. The best time would be when Mamu would enter, bringing all kinds of spicy treats to go with our sugary delights.

I loved Sundays. This had been our routine when

Mom was alive, and we did not want to change something that was so good.

Mamu would occasionally take Selma and me out on Sunday afternoons, or on Friday after prayers. We would either go to see some funny movie in the theater, or he would take us on an historical tour of the city.

Lucknow is filled with beautiful palaces and monuments like the Bara Imaambara, the majestic clock tower, the Akbari gate, and the Gomati river flowing through the middle of the city. I most loved going to the Imaambara; it had such huge sprawling lawns, gardens, fountains, and beautiful flowers. The monument itself is a wonder: it was actually a place of worship for the Shia Muslims, and was built by Nawab Asaf-Ud-Daula, a Mughal prince, in 1783.

This monument is an architectural wonder. Built in the time of the great famine, it provided employment to thousands. I felt like a princess, walking through its magnificent hallways, and lying down to gaze into its alluring domes. Selma and I would play for many hours there, and Mamu would lie dozing under some shady tree.

When Baba was sad, he would go for a quiet walk on the shores of the Gomati. It was beautiful at sunset. Mamu would babysit us till Dad finally came home.

It had been around two years since Mom had left us. Baba hardly spoke anymore. He just went to work and back. We ate dinner quietly. I felt I was living with a shadow. There was something missing in the house. I kept thinking about life with Mom – her selfless love, never-tiring care for us and her tenderness. I took a deep breath through my heap of emotions, and what I inhaled back was the sweet smell of the champa. I had found a way of keeping Mom alive, and Baba too.

Next day, on our way back from school, Selma and I stopped at the flower market and bought some champa flowers. As I held them in my palm, uncontrollable tears rolled down my cheeks. I looked at Selma helplessly, with tear-filled eyes, and said, "I miss her, how will I live without her?" That evening, I went home and put some of the champa under Baba's pillow, and some under mine.

After dinner, Baba went to bed early. I stayed up, thinking of Mom and her sweet-smelling memories. I heard a knock on my door. It was Baba. He had discovered the flowers.

He had this strange, expectant look on his face,

as if to say, "Was she here?" I just lifted my pillow and showed him the flowers under my pillow. Baba smiled for the first time after many months.

He came near me and placed his hands lovingly on my head, and said, "God bless you." Every day after that, either I or Baba would bring the flowers home and let my mother's fragrance make us smile and live again.

It was during these days that Baba started bringing Yusuf home every evening. We would have dinner together and then a poetry session. I listened on, as I washed the dishes and cleaned the kitchen. I was very grateful to Yusuf for making Baba smile again.

Yusuf was a very intelligent man. He always knew what to say and when to say it. He could wade through people's weakness, and enter their hearts. Baba needed such council then, and Yusuf, the master-mind that he was, knew this very well. I would always confide my problems to Yusuf; he had become like a middle-man between Baba and me. I became more comfortable with him than I had ever been with any man. I began to trust him.

There were rumors in the community that Yusuf would charm young girls with his poems, and had quite a number of flings.

When asked about this, he would always dismiss it as, "Nothing serious."

These days Mamu was very busy, because his wife was finally pregnant. Mamu was on top of the world. He spent most of his time at home, planning for the baby or training his pigeons.

6

It was Tuesday, and Selma and I were waiting outside our school for Baban to pick us up. He had become very old, but to make some extra bucks he would still pick up some other customers when we were at school. Raffia was of marriageable age, and the stress of the dowry was really killing poor Baban. Baba trusted him so much that he even helped him to buy a motorized rickshaw, so that he could continue to bring us home.

It was 6:30 pm and Baban wasn't there yet. Selma was very restless; she knew her dad would be furious if his dinner wasn't ready on time. She pleaded with me, "Let's start walking, we might find Baban on our way." Our house was only about two blocks away. We started to walk; we could hear the sound of the evening call for prayer – *Azaan*. The sun was slipping behind the branches of the huge *pipal* tree.

I tried to make small talk with Selma. I knew she was very tense, but she kept pulling my hand and trying to make me walk faster. I wished I had not worn my new sandals today, they were not meant for fast walking. Suddenly, Selma stopped in the middle of a small intersection and started to look around. "What?" I said, "I thought you knew the way."

"Yeah, I do, but I also know this narrow lane father takes sometimes when he needs to get home soon. There it is, Hasnabad Lane. Let's take that," Selma pointed.

As we skirted down the lane, the sounds of our footsteps seemed to echo against the cramped-up houses. This was a back alley where people often left their garbage to be picked up by the street sweeper. The stench of the garbage made me want to throw up. Selma saw me and gave me her handkerchief to cover my nose. A hundred feet down, Selma and I saw a group of young boys loitering around. They seemed too loud and wild. We nervously passed their group, me clenching Selma's sweaty palm as tight as I could, until we were stopped in our tracks by Yaqoob. He lived a few blocks from us, and we knew him because he was always getting into trouble with the police. My father had often seen him in court.

Yaqoob stared insidiously into my eyes, his foul tobacco breath was choking me, and then his hands touched my hair. I thought I would faint any minute. He smiled, and I could see his tarnished teeth, filled with gunk from *paan* (Indian betel leaf) which he was always chewing. His breath came so close to me, I felt as if my face had been pushed into a pile of garbage. I closed my eyes in fear. Suddenly I could smell the sweet fragrance of jasmine oil. I opened my eyes to see that now I was staring at the back of Selma's oily head.

Like a swift wind, Selma had rushed in front of me, yelling, "Leave her alone, and give us way, or else!" She couldn't think of anything that could scare Yaqoob. All the boys laughed and teased Yaqoob that he should now start to shiver before two girls. Yaqoob sniggered; his tobacco-chewing dirty teeth and breath came too close to Selma's face.

In a split second, Selma gave him a resounding slap, grabbed my hand and said, "Run!" We ran as if there was a tsunami following us. Yaqoob was stunned; he composed himself and began to chase us, and at that very moment I saw four middle-aged men walking down our street. They had noticed the commotion, and thus had increased their pace to get to us. Yaqoob's friends warned him about the oncoming trouble, and they pulled him away and ran off into a dusty small alley. Selma told me to cover my face with my scarf.

She said, "These men shouldn't see our faces, or else they could inform our parents, and that would really embarrass our folks." As we passed by the four men, they kept trying to talk to us. Selma pulled my hand and said, "Keep walking, don't stop to talk." Selma knew that in our conservative community, people make up stories very easily to defame girls. I agreed with Selma's fears, for I too knew that in our world a girl's character is like a piece of crystal – even the tiniest scar would be considered a flaw, thus making her worthless.

As we reached the main road, we slowed down. It was, as usual, swarming with people. I was never so happy to see so many unknown faces. When we reached Selma's house, Selma wiped her sweaty face with her scarf, very calmly put her hand on my shoulder, and said, "Don't mention this to anyone." I felt like a little child listening to her mother. Selma always had that effect on me. She was always in control and I would just let life happen to me.

Baba was home early with Yusuf. They had picked

up some kabobs and naan from the marketplace and were chatting loudly about some new poet they had heard recite on the street. I silently entered the kitchen. I opened the fridge and poured myself a cold glass of water. As I gently sipped it, my sweat condensed, and my clothes began to stick to me. I told Baba I was going for a bath. My heart was echoing with the sounds of Yaqoob's sniggering and Selma's slap.

The cold water running down my spine awakened me, and I remembered Selma's words, "Don't mention this to anyone." I composed myself to look as normal as I could and went into the kitchen to serve dinner. After dinner I cleaned the kitchen and Yusuf came in to say goodbye.

He looked at my pale face and said, "Everything okay?" He gently touched my face with the back of his hand and said, "My God, you are freezing. You girls need to eat more, you are too delicate."

Yusuf picked up the last kabob and said, "No one makes them as good as Tunda, he's too good. Good night, dear."

Finally I was all alone. Yusuf had left and I could hear Baba walk to his room.

I stood there in the kitchen silently and let my tears

roll down my cheeks. I had kept Selma's promise even though I was yearning to at least tell Yusuf about it. I felt proud, like an obedient child.

Since Mom passed away, Baba had become very distant from me. We hardly spoke; he always appeared to be engrossed in one of his legal cases or some poetry. I knew that he was just doing this to avoid being empty-minded; he knew that thoughts of Mom would come and make him fall apart. But every night when Baba entered his bedroom, he would finally surrender to the sweet fragrance of the champa flower.

Baba's distance bought Yusuf close to me. Maybe Yusuf wanted to lighten Baba's pain and loneliness, or maybe he was just toying with our emotions. Today I have realized that I was just a brief source of inspiration for him, and nothing more.

I wish I had realized this then and not taken his attention and care as love, so that my heart wouldn't have been scarred forever.

7

We were in our final year of college. Studies and household chores kept me very busy, but still every evening I would find myself very alone. I would sit outside my kitchen and watch the people happily going home and the hustle and bustle of children playing their games. It was after few months that I realized I was waiting outside every evening, in the hope that Yusuf would drop by and the house would come alive again.

One such evening I waited a very long time on my doorstep, the breeze was perfect, and I actually dozed off a little. I smelt a sharp, sweet aroma: *keewam*, a very familiar smell. It was a kind of mouth freshener made of rose petals and a little tobacco. Yusuf loved to chew on it. When I opened my eyes I saw Yusuf sitting next to me in a white kurta pajama. Smiling away impishly at me, he said, "Whose thoughts lull you, dear one?" For the first time that day I saw a strange sparkle in his eyes; he looked deep into my eyes, as if he could read my thoughts, smiled as if he knew that his charm was working on me. I was blinded, blinded by the bright rays of love.

Yusuf patted my shoulder and said, "Let's go and check on Baba."

The next few days at college my heart was much burdened. I kept thinking of what Selma had done for me. She had saved me from being humiliated by Yaqoob, and now that I thought of it, she had saved me from harm and disgrace. Just at the thought of what would have happened if Selma had not been with me at that moment would send shivers down my spine. Yaqoob and his friends could have destroyed me.

I admired Selma's courage; I don't think I would ever have the strength to do something like what Selma had done, even to save my own life. I was a very timid person without any courage and she knew that, but she didn't consider this to be a bad thing. She accepted me as I was, with both my goodness and my weakness.

Baba, due to his professional status, had better income than Selma's father. I would often buy Selma things that I knew she liked, but for her it was always a needless expense. We both had the same shoe and clothing sizes. I would often let her borrow my pretty rhinestones sandals that she loved so much, or my clothes; even though they hung on her slightly, she loved them so. She didn't mind wearing them. We were more like sisters than friends. To make it up to me, sometime she could cook my favorite dishes, like *nahari* or *zarda*, and she would quietly sneak it to me through my back kitchen door. It was always enough just for me, and as she sweetly put it, it's only for you.

I knew things were quite shallow, money-wise, in Selma's house. My favorite gift to her was taking her to the sweet shop across from our college. After the attack, I decided, to lessen the weight in my heart and to casually thank Selma for saving me, I would take her to the sweet shop.

8

Santosh Sweet Mart, or the local *halwaii*, was owned by Santosh. He was around fifty-five years old, and was married to a beautiful twenty-eight-year-old girl called Razia. Santosh's only employee was Hari, who did most of the cooking, and Razia helped him. Santosh just sat around with his big fat belly on the cash counter. We parked our rickshaw a little away from the shop, so that we would have a little privacy from all the men that crowded around the shop. Baban would kindly go and place our requests, then bring the treats back to us in the rickshaw. I would always order extra, for Raffia and her brother Baban's children, which Baban accepted very humbly.

Selma's most favorite dish was fresh hot sweet jalebees with chilled fresh cream. The cream in India is very thick and very high in fat, made from buffalo's milk. Lucknow was famous for its fresh, luxurious cream, known as malai.

The cream is taken from freshly boiled milk, then cooled in a steel container over ice. Later it is transferred to small earthen bowls called *secora*. Finally, these secoras are placed over ice, for chilling. Earthen bowls are used because they give a very sweet flavor and aroma to the cream or the rice pudding. It smelled like the fragrance of the first rain. Selma's order would go jalebees, malai, and fresh hot samosas. I would just have some hot condensed milk that had been mixed with crushed almonds, pistachios and sugar.

Every morning Hari would wash this immensely huge pot called a *kadai*. He would then place this huge vessel on a charcoal stove, and pour in about 10 liters of fresh buffalo milk, just brought from the dairy next door. The milk had to be cooked for hours to be reduced to the desired thickness. A little sugar, almonds, pistachios and saffron would be added just before serving. Lucknow was very pompous in its culture. The city used to be ruled by Nawabs, or princes, and so the people tried to maintain that royal culture, even after the estates were taken over by the government.

Selma started munching right away, and elaborately narrating the immense delight that she was getting from her snack. I on the other hand, sipped the milk very slowly, inhaling the glory of the happiness that I had just given Selma. Amidst all this glory, an intense guilt stung my heart. I knew that this was no reward for what Selma had done for me. It was a sheer act of selfless courage, and no amount or kind of reward was worthy of it. The whole incident brought tears of shame to my eyes – was I trying to reward Selma for her bravery, or was I trying to hide my lack of courage? I knew I could have never done what Selma had done for me.

Selma noticed my watering eyes, and asked if something was wrong. I just smiled and said that the milk was too hot.

She said "don't burn your pretty lips"; but it wasn't my lips that were burning up, but rather my soul.

I realized that I had always tried to buy Selma's friendship. I was weak and timid, and she was strong. I needed her. I wished and wished I could be like her, but life had another script written out for me.

All these feelings of guilt were not as strong as the hormones churning inside me. They made me more vulnerable to Yusuf's charm. Every day after college and finishing my chores, my eyes and heart would

Unspoken

wait anxiously for his footsteps.

9

YUSUF

Yusuf, well, he was the true personification of manhood. He was about six feet in height, and was very fair-skinned. His face was marred with the marks of a smallpox episode, but they only made his face look more rough and rugged. He had very bushy eyebrows, deep set hazelnut eyes, a very straight nose, thick pink lips and a very demanding chin.

The part of his face that I liked best, was a deep cleft which ran through the middle of his chin. He also had a distinctive split in his left ear lobe from a childhood squabble, in which his friend had injured his ear with a shaving blade. Yusuf weighed around 160 lbs., was in great, muscular shape, and had thick curly hair, which I always wanted to run my fingers through. To me, and a lot of girls my age, he was like someone straight from a romance novel. When he spoke, his husky voice could send chills of thrill through young hearts. I think he could make anyone melt. Yusuf was about forty-six and I was twenty-one.

No matter where I was in the house, I knew the second he came into my home. As soon as his fragrance entered my breath, my whole body would shiver with excitement, and I could actually feel my face glowing. I would hide for a moment, till I could conceal the colors on my face, and then face him casually. He would always know; he would smile and say, "You are glowing today. Don't waste your charms on me; I'm already under your spell." I would shy away from this fact, that he could read every emotion through my eyes, and thus had more control over my weak, inexperienced heart. His greatest gift was that he always knew what to say and when, as if he could read minds. I was like putty in his hands.

The last few weeks of college were very challenging, not only due to studies and Yusuf, but because Selma had told me that Yaqoob was loitering around her house. He had sent her a love letter through the *chaiwala* or the canteen boy. She thought that he had gone mad. She had slapped and insulted him, and now he was proclaiming that he had been awakened with love for her? She said she always hated him, because he was a street rat, with no culture, education or future. Selma was very threatened by this crazy behavior of Yaqoob. If ever her father saw Yaqoob, and knew his intentions, he would kill him – or kill Selma.

I wanted to tell Yusuf about this. I thought maybe Yusuf could scare Yaqoob off. Selma thought I was very childish, because according to her, Yusuf himself was a good for nothing guy. She had heard many stories about his various flings with young girls. After that day, I never mentioned Yusuf to Selma again.

I knew I was playing with fire, but it seemed so irresistible and exciting. What I didn't realize was that the fire, too, was playing with me, and it would definitely burn me; I was naive then. As my life was getting more and more entangled with Yusuf, Selma's life was a constant state of anxiety.

A week later, Mamu's wife gave birth to a chubby little boy. Mamu named him Sheraz. The baby brought happiness to all of us. It was so nice to see Mamu so enthralled. God had really blessed him, and I felt that Mamu deserved the best of best, because he was a wonderful human being. When Mamu brought the baby to our home, Baba would change completely. Both men would act like little children, trying to bring a smile to Sheraz's sweet lips.

I was too scared to tell Mamu anything about my or Selma's life, as I didn't have the heart to spoil his joy. Maybe I was too guilty, and didn't have the courage to confess.

10

Yaqoob kept a close watch on Selma all the time, and would follow her everywhere. This was his way of showing Selma that he could not forget what she had done to him, not that he had become such a love puppy. Yaqoob's love was only a drama to entertain his friends.

Some evenings, I would go over to Selma's house to do our homework. I would often see Yaqoob standing across her house. He always dressed so loud and garishly. He wore tight, drainpipe-like pants, which were at least two sizes too small for him, and they looked obscene. His shirt was also tight fitted, colorful and unbuttoned to his navel, and his mouth dripped with paan and tobacco. Yaqoob always tied a handkerchief around his neck, which he thought made him look cool. He was quite dark in complexion, had thick, untidy hair, and wore gaudy shoes.

He looked so conceited standing there in all his finery, but to everyone, he looked like a real ruffian.

Yaqoob's father had passed away in a car accident when Yaqoob was only six. He had no siblings; he lived with his ailing mother. Yaqoob had left school when his father passed away. Since then, he took care of himself and his mother by doing odd jobs, which were mostly illegal in nature. He was around twenty now, but he had already visited the jail about six times. Since his father's death, Yaqoob had hung out with this gang of five friends that led him into a number of dishonest acts.

Selma was the first girl he had encountered in his life. Before this he was too occupied with stealing and making a quick buck. It was the first time that he had been slapped by a girl, in front of his peers. This insult had to be corrected, and soon. To accomplish this, he softly paddled his friends into believing that he was in love with Selma, that she had become the spice in his bland life.

It was only a few days later that Yaqoob found the opportunity he was looking for. Yaqoob had been informed by some of his friends that Selma's father was going on a business trip to Kanpur. It was a Friday afternoon when Yaqoob saw Selma's step mom leave for her prayer at the mosque with her son, as they always did. Yaqoob knew that Selma would be alone at home. He kept his friends on guard around the house. It was around 1:30 pm and the streets were desolate. There were some wooden boxes kept in Selma's backyard. Yaqoob climbed over the piled boxes and broke in through the glass pane of Selma's bathroom window. He slithered through the opening, and landed in the bathtub.

He found Selma asleep in her room. Yaqoob pleaded with her to talk to him. Selma was terrified to see him inside her house. She ran like a scared bird. She yelled for help, but it being a Friday, most people were either at the mosque or taking an afternoon nap. She gathered all her courage and ordered him to leave her house. Yaqoob insisted that she had to listen to what he had to say to her. She attacked him with whatever she could lay her hands on, but Yaqoob could not be deterred. He caught Selma, and pulled her really close to him. In a fit of fury, Selma slapped Yaqoob and pushed him down. Yaqoob hit his head on the end of the marble table. He felt blood oozing out from his wound. He looked at the blood, and then looked at Selma. His eyes began to reflect the color of blood. Selma knew she had stepped on the snake.

This was the last straw that broke Yaqoob's goodness. He dragged Selma onto her bed, and forced himself on her. He raped her repeatedly, like a wild animal devours his prey. After nearly an hour, when Selma could not bear the pain anymore, she lost consciousness. Yaqoob panicked; he left Selma lying there half dead and fled from the house the same way he came in.

His friends were still obediently waiting for him outside. They found Yaqoob looking very flushed and scared. He was terrified; his heart was pounding with the thought that he might have killed Selma. He refused to tell his friends anything. They all began to congratulate him on his victory. Yaqoob's flushed face gave out his secret. The only thing that he skipped telling his friends was that it was not love, but rape, which he had just performed.

Yaqoob washed himself up from a leaking street faucet, and chewed a heavy load of tobacco. After he cooled down, he realized he had to take control of himself and act calm. When his friends asked him what Selma had to say, he blatantly smiled and said, "She loves me too, and you will see how she will come running to me." Even as he said this, he prayed that she would come to him.

When Selma gained consciousness, it took her a while to realize what had happened to her. She tried to get up from her bed, but her feet felt like jelly; she couldn't walk. She fell on the floor and sank into unconsciousness again.

That evening when Selma's mom finally returned from her groceries, she found Selma's bedroom door closed. She assumed that Selma had gone to sleep early, so that she didn't have to help out with the household chores. Her stepmother started to shower abuses at the closed door behind which Selma lay, soaked in tears, sweat and blood. Selma yearned for her real mom, and her dear friend Sharmeen. She stayed on her bedroom floor the whole night, weeping in pain, shame, and hopelessness.

The next morning Selma had a bath and washed off all the grime that Yaqoob had left on her. With herculean effort, she got dressed, and composed herself to face her family. Her face looked scarred from the consuming crying. She went straight to the kitchen and started her daily chores. Selma had to look as normal as possible, even though her legs were still shaking, and it felt as if she had come out of a grave illness. What had happened to her was as if it was her own fate. She, like many other girls in our society, took it as her destiny. She couldn't tell anyone about it, not even her parents. She knew that her father would die of shame, and her step-mom would either throw her out of her house or kill her.

She told her mom that she had to study for some big test, and wasn't going to college. Selma didn't have enough courage to go out and face the world, or face Yaqoob, who she feared would be brazenly standing outside.

That day, I was supposed to meet Selma at the college library to study, but Selma didn't show up. I waited, finished my studying and then left. On my way back I decided to call on Selma. I rang the doorbell, no one answered, and I assumed Selma might have gone out with her step-mom for some errands.

Monday was our final exam and Selma still didn't turn up. I knew now that something was drastically wrong, as Selma would never miss her final paper. All kinds of negative happenings passed my mind, as to what could have happened. But never in my scariest dreams could I have ever imagined the gory tale that Selma was about to tell me. When I reached Selma's house, I rang the doorbell again and again, but no answer. Finally I started walking to the backyard of the house, from there I could peep through Selma's bedroom window. I saw Selma lying on her bed. I started to knock frantically on her window; I was scared that she was sick.

A mask of intense fear covered Selma's face when I knocked at her window. I had startled her. As soon as she let me in, she collapsed. There was no one else at home at that time. I ran to the kitchen brought some water and washed her face. Selma revived, but she soon fell into my lap like a helpless child and burst into weeping. I started asking her why she had missed her finals. Selma didn't answer for a while. Suddenly she took control of herself, had a drink of water, and began to talk. She asked me how my exam went and said that she was so happy to see me.

Selma looked as though she had aged ten years in these few days. When I begged Selma to tell me what had happened, she started to narrate that gory incident in such detail that it made me sick to my stomach. I wanted to just shut her mouth– why was she talking of such unthinkable things? This couldn't have happened to my dearest friend, this couldn't have happened to anyone. My most unimaginable fear had come true, my brain shut down; I fainted.

When I recovered, I was lying on Selma's bed and Selma was putting cold compresses on my forehead. It all seemed like a bad dream, as if Selma had not said anything to me. I kissed her hands with intense affection, and said, "You are all right, you are safe."

Selma pressed my hand like a mother consoles her daughter, smiled and said, "I'm fine, I'll be all right, you don't worry about anything." Then she said, looking deep into my anxious eyes, "Promise me you will not repeat these things to anyone in your life, and that no one should ever know about this." That's when I realized that this was not a bad dream but a horrific piece of reality. I was so afraid; I told Selma I would keep this secret buried in my heart.

Still, I could not entirely hide my fear from Selma. "What if you get pregnant? What if he has infected you with some illness? After all he was a mere roadside rat."

Selma tried very hard to hide the fear that these questions had brought, and said, "We'll just have to wait and see. Every wound heals, and this too will heal one day."

Selma had once again shielded me from pain and fear. As I was leaving, I met Selma's dad on the way out. He greeted me and asked me if we both had done well in our finals. That's when I realized that Selma had not told anyone about the incident, except me. Walking back home I kept chanting Selma's promise in my head that I was not to tell anyone about this. I realized that I had very sincerely accepted her plea.

This made me question myself: why was I so eager to hide what had happened to Selma? Was it because of Selma, or was it because I knew in my heart that I was the reason that had led Selma to these horrible eventualities. This thought was driving me insane. With all my courage I tried desperately to erase it from my mind. I wanted to believe that nothing had happened and all was well. As I entered my house I wiped off every emotion from my face. I could hear Yusuf and Baba chatting in the study. I started setting dinner on the table; I was late, and they were hungry. Yusuf got ready to leave; he explained that his mother always complained that she often has to eat dinner alone. My eyes pleaded with Yusuf, and he stayed. Baba saw my swollen eyes and knew I had been crying, but after Mom's death, Baba just didn't want to face or share any more pain.

11

After dinner, Yusuf helped me clean up. Baba went to his room, as he knew Yusuf would deal with my problem.

That day I desperately wished that Baba was strong, and it could have been his shoulder that I could weep on. Yusuf, however, tried to find out what was wrong, but how could I tell him; I myself wasn't ready to accept Selma's reality. Yusuf cornered me near the fridge, and as my back touched the cold metal surface, a chill went through me. I didn't know if this was because of the cold steel, or Yusuf being so close to me. He looked deep into my eyes and gently ran his finger on my cheeks. I froze for a moment, and he kissed me, he kept kissing me frantically. Finally I gathered strength and pushed him away. I ran to my room, banged the door, and then I surrendered to my weak body and fell into a deep sleep.

Next morning as I was getting ready to go to Selma's house, I looked at myself in the mirror. My lips reminded me of Yusuf and last night. They didn't look different. I ran my finger over my lips, they felt the same; well, I had never felt my lips before today. I had never wanted Yusuf to get physical with me. I loved him, I needed him, but I did not know what Yusuf had wanted from me. My mind snapped my heart; because this was no time for passion, it was time for compassion. Selma needed me, and I had to do anything to make her feel better. Life was really stretching Selma's courage, and as her best friend I could not leave her alone.

When I reached her house Selma was trying wearily to be her old self again. She told me that her dad had informed them last night that they had to move to Hyderabad, as he was posted back there again.

"We will be moving within a month," she said. Her mom was very happy, because she never liked Lucknow.

I caught Selma's hand as she rushed by and asked, "How are you going to live there alone?"

She replied, "Well, I'll never be alone! You will always be there in my heart and mind to keep me alive." We hugged each other very intensely, as if no amount of distance could make us feel that we were apart.

I wanted to tell Selma about Yusuf, but I did not think the time was right, so I kept quiet. I knew that if I did tell Selma, she would definitely go and kill Yusuf, and I didn't want her to do that. I loved Yusuf, no matter how he was, and I never wanted him to get hurt.

For the next few weeks Selma was busy with her packing, and Yaqoob still kept shamelessly appearing every day at her door. Sometimes when I saw him, I would actually feel my hands moving towards my sandals, so that I could hit him with them. I wished that God had blessed me with that courage. I would dream that I was hitting Yaqoob, tearing his clothes, throwing him in the mud, and smearing his face with dirt. It exhausted me even to dream about it, but it always felt so good that I would feel proud of myself.

I hated Yaqoob so much that it would make me nauseous. I had to train myself not to see him, as if he did not exist. After Selma's intense emotion drenching me, I could not go home yet.

Whenever I was lost, I would go to Mamu's house. That day my feet drew me towards his house. Mamu was home; he was busy in the backyard, feeding his pigeons. Mamu's biggest passion was to breed and train pigeons. There were pigeon competitions in Lucknow as a part of the pompous culture that Lucknow was engulfed in.

I would often come and help Mamu take care of his birds. Mamu had lovingly named each one. There was Iqbal his favorite, the most strong, intelligent, and good-looking. Then there was Sami, Feroz, Dilruba, amongst the many others. Mamu had noticed that I was very upset, and while he never asked what was wrong, he always tried to cheer me up. Once I was happy, he knew I would spill the beans easily.

That day Mamu told me that he had a surprise for me, and asked me to wait outside. He went in the pigeon coop, and came out with the most amazing thing I had ever seen. It was a snow-white pigeon. These pigeons were very expensive, and Mamu had been saving for a while to get one. I had never seen a bird so white. She had deep grey eyes, and a very fancy, Chinese fan-shaped tail.

Mamu put her on my shoulder. She at once began to tickle my ears and muttered into them. I knew she belonged to me, and loved me. But I was scared to handle her at first, for I knew she was very expensive.

Mamu told me, "If you love her, and take good care of her, that would be enough for me." I hugged Mamu, and wept bitterly, but I still could not tell Mamu what had happened.

Mamu didn't push me, he was just happy for the time being that he was able to wipe my tears. He would always tell me, "It feels nice to make you smile, for I know there may be many tears in your life which I may not be able to erase."

We had to name this new bird, and I knew of a name right away: Lucky. I was Mamu's little pigeon, and I felt very lucky to have him in my life. Mamu had kept my faith in humanity and goodness alive. Mamu's nickname for me was *chirdia*, a little birdie like a sparrow.

We played with Lucky for hours. Mamu taught me how to train her, so that when we called out to her in a special whistle tone, she would come and land straight on my shoulder.

I was scared to let go of her, because I feared she wouldn't come back to me. Mamu told me, "Feed her, caress her, she will know you love her, and she will return to you. After all, that's all anyone needs."

It was hard work, but I was willing to test whether love was one of my strengths. I never realized that

Waheeda Soomro

life was teaching me a precious lesson: if you love something, let it go, and if it loves you, it will come back to you. I wish I had been listening carefully to the whispers of wisdom; I could have saved myself so much pain.

12

When I reached home, I saw Baban sitting on our front porch; he looked very frantic and scared. His kurta was soaking in sweat; his feet were bare, dry and dusty. He looked so petrified, as if he had been burnt by life. I asked him what was wrong. He said only that he needed to speak to my father. I went in and got him a glass of cold water and some bread. Baba wasn't home yet, and Baban waited outside till he came. When Baba returned, he called Baban inside his study. The doors were shut, and they spoke for quite a while.

After Baban left, Baba came inside very scared and pale. I offered Baba a glass of water and inquired why he looked so dejected. Then he explained to me that Baban's daughter Raffia's fiancé, that forty-year-old man had demanded that Baban pay him a dowry of 25,000 rupees. Baban over the years had collected

20,000 but even after selling off all his worldly belongings he could not come up with the rest of the money. Baban had come to apologize to Baba, because that morning he had to sell the rickshaw which Baba had given him for our transportation. He then went on to narrate that Baban paid the man the money, and fixed the marriage date.

But Baban had a big shock waiting for him when he reached home. Raffia had hung herself, and died a few hours before he returned. She left a letter for her father. "Baba I am your daughter, but all I have been is a constant burden on you and Mom, and I want you to remember me as your daughter and not as your burden. I am killing myself, so that you don't have to kill yourself for that worthless, greedy man. Your life is very precious to me, you have been a great father to me, and I love you and respect you immensely. I am hoping that my death will be a lesson to other fathers and men, so that one day this inhumane system of dowry may end. Daughters are as important as sons. Treat them as your strength, and not as your weakness. Forgive me if I have wronged you."

Baba walked all heartbroken to his room, and shut the door. I wiped my tears, and Raffia's last words kept coming back to me. Somehow I knew she had done the right thing. There is a reason why God has made women stronger than men, and that is because we would be expected to make all the sacrifices in this world. No matter how time passes and how often civilization changes, women will get the rawest deal, and we are expected to cope with it, or at least not be an obstruction for the men.

I knew then, that I too could not be a problem for my father; I had fallen in love, but with the wrong man, and at the wrong age. In our community arranged marriages are the fate of the good child. I had not heard of any love marriages in our entire family or social circle. We were not given the liberty to fall in love; since we were naive, we could not see what was good or bad for our future. We were given an understanding that parents knew everything; after all, they had lived and experienced life. What people often wouldn't understand is that, *"love is like a natural occurrence, one cannot predict it or stop it."* Frankly, there was nothing in my life that I could decide for myself. Parents would decide, or destiny. I knew that, in our social system, I had committed a crime by loving Yusuf, and this I would have to hold unspoken in my heart forever. If I was going to suffer, it would be all my doing, and I would just have to live with this guilt of falling in love. I could never cross my threshold and confess my love to Yusuf, and never, never to my father; it would be disgraceful.

I could not dare to disturb the plans and dreams that my father had for me. His life and name could not be marred by anyone, especially not by his daughter. This made me wonder whether my mother had held any secrets in her heart. We would always talk about how Baba struggled, how he worked so hard to get here. He would tell us detailed stories about his childhood, and we would hear them again and again. No one ever asked Mom about her childhood, and she never spoke about her past. I felt so angry at myself because I too never encouraged her, no matter if she had achieved anything in her life or not, she was still a human being, she was my mother. It was too late for me now, for my mom was gone, and she had taken all her pains, dreams, and secrets to her grave.

Mothers are like little dictionaries that we carry in our hearts forever. "Do this, this will help you; don't do this, it will hurt you." But we know so little about what secrets lie behind those caring eyes.

I went into Baba's room, and sat down beside

him on his bed. I told him that I wished we could have known Baban better and we should have asked him if he had any problems. He was a part of this household, and yet we were so distant from him. I kept talking, as if I was trying to drain my loss, of not being able to be more humane. Baba was fast asleep, he hadn't heard a word I said, but I had recognized another weakness of mine: *"in this race to be perfect, and accepted, we have stopped being humane...Is this what we call, civilization?"*

13

August 11 was the day Selma was moving. There was such a hustle bustle in her house for the next few days. The packing had made Selma assume her old self again, taking charge of everything. Selma's parents were quite lost without her. After all, she was the one that did all the work. I would go over every day to help her. Occasionally we would just sit down exhausted, and look at each other with so much to say, then evade it by getting back to the task at hand.

One night, I invited Selma's family to a lavish farewell dinner at my home. I cooked everything Selma loved, and I cooked it with a great deal of love. I was going to miss her immensely. The question I was avoiding asking myself was, "Will I be able to even live without her?" I couldn't let Selma know of my insecurities; she had enough on her conscience already. That night at dinner Selma was happy, or at least was trying her best to look that way. There was so much life in the house. Suddenly the doorbell rang, and it was Yusuf. We had not invited him because I knew Selma didn't like him, and I didn't want Selma to be suspicious that there was anything serious between us.

Yusuf joined us for dinner, and Selma became uncomfortable right away. I don't know why I was hiding this from her. I guess I knew I was wrong, and knew that she would yell at me for being such a sap. But I was drenched in Yusuf's love so deeply that my mind was numbed. The feeling of being in love was so amazing that I didn't let my sanity prevail.

The next day we all went to drop Selma and her family at the train station. Baba called Yusuf to help us go to the station. Yusuf could not bring his car, which was having some trouble. But he couldn't refuse the offer to accompany us. We hired a rickshaw in which Selma, Yusuf, and I sat together. I had not realized the power of Selma's insightful thinking.

Suddenly, in the middle of the journey, she looked defiantly into Yusuf's face and said, "Stop whatever you are trying to do to my friend, I know you can only give her pain. If you do not stop, I will put a stop to it, and then you will be ashamed and unmasked amongst the very people who think you are a good person."

I was trembling with shock. I thought Yusuf would slap her. Selma kept glaring at him, waiting for an answer, but Yusuf just smirked at her, and said, "You worry too much, your friend is too precious to me."

We held hands tightly, me and Selma, till the train arrived to take her away from me. All the time Selma kept wiping my tears and saying, "I'm only going to be a few hours away from you, you can come to me anytime, and I'll come too." As she took her hand away from me to get on the train, I felt a very vast distance developing between us, it created a hollow feeling deep inside me. Later I would realize that it wasn't just the train taking her away, but life would be taking her beyond measurable distances away from me.

I felt so torn between Selma, Yusuf, and Baba, and that deep hollow inside me made me feel weaker. On the way back home Yusuf was very caring towards me. He looked very happy, and for the first time I felt that he loved me, even though he had never said it in words. I felt relieved as well that I had forgiven Yusuf for kissing me. I could not be mad with him too long. But back then what I had not realized was that no amount of forgiveness or love would compensate for the immense pain that I would be carrying within me forever.

Selma's absence was another excuse for me to get closer and closer to Yusuf, not that I didn't have other friends. The truth was I couldn't resist Yusuf's charm, and most of all, I was enjoying his admiration. He would always say that I inspired him. He would write a new poem for me, about me, every day. One of his poems, describing the beauty of my face, I remember word for word till today. The day after he wrote it, some friends asked him to read one of his new poems, and he read the poem about my face. When he told me this, I was so cross at him for doing so – it was too personal, and it belonged only to me. He could not share it with anyone.

I made him give me all the poems he wrote about me. He wrote them all down, but did not sign under them. Today, when I look back, maturity tells me that he was merely enacting a role of a lover, and that he never did love me. It was always all about him, never about me or anyone else. Yusuf, I feel, was a type of narcissist. He used people as inspiration, and then threw them away like a piece of paper.

I remember in one of his poems he had said, "Your love imprisons me forever, and I shall be me alone till eternity." Now when I read that line again, I know that he was not saying this about himself, but that I would be imprisoned in his love forever.

Some people say it is better to have loved and lost, than to never have loved at all. But how can one lose in love? It is not a battle or a game, or at least it wasn't for me. One can only love, and then love some more. I really believed in this myth that love never dies; I kept it alive in the depths of my heart for twenty-five years and clung to it, I wouldn't let it die.

14

BABA

A few weeks after Selma left we received a letter from Uncle Shabir in England. I was waiting for Baba eagerly. I knew he always awaited his brother's letters. After Mom passed away, Baba and Uncle Shabir became very close. Sometimes they would speak late into the night.

At 7:30 pm Baba finally arrived. He was late, flustered, and sweating profusely. He looked very agitated. He just flopped in one of the chairs and asked for a glass of water. When I returned with the water, he gulped it down at once. I had never seen Baba in this frame of mind; to me he looked very angry. I asked him if he was feeling all right.

He wiped his sweat, smiled at me, and said, "I'm fine, I'll just go and take a bath, and then we can eat."

After dinner I gave him the letter. There was a glow of hope on his face, he read it and looked so relieved, as if his prayers had been answered. There was a photograph in the letter, which Baba stared at for a moment, then he put it back carefully in the envelope. That night Baba called Shabir, and they spoke for a long time. Next morning I was surprised when Baba told me that he wasn't going to work, and that he had an important engagement at home. I brought Baba his tea in the study, and as I was leaving he called out to me and asked me sit next to him.

Baba had never made such a gesture before. He held my hand fondly, and said, "I love you a lot, and no matter what anyone says or does you will always be most precious to me. I'm sorry I have neglected you, and left you alone after you lost your mother. I should have given you more attention, but don't worry, now I'll take care of everything."

I couldn't understand what he was talking about, but it felt good. I had always wanted to hear this from him. The doorbell rang.

I got up, and Baba held my hand and said, "I'll get it. I want you to go to your room and stay there." Now I was really scared, but not in my wildest thoughts could I have conceived what was about to happen.

It was Yusuf, who had come to see Baba. I heard

his voice and my heart sank, I thought I was going to faint; suddenly everything that Baba had just said to me was coming into context. I couldn't resist and I slightly cracked open my door, so that I could hear them. Baba's voice sounded very hurt and emotional. I heard him say, "Yusuf, you know, when I first got acquainted with you, people had warned me that you were a wild one, you chased girls and were very fancy free. But I saw some goodness in you, and I wanted to keep that alive. Of course I needed a friend too, and you fitted the slip. To be very honest, Yusuf, you charmed me too, just like everyone else. I began to enjoy your company, and I invited you into my home, to be a part of my family."

Baba continued, "My friends were right, and I was a fool, because I left my most precious belonging unguarded and like an eagle you snatched her. I think in this whole community I was the only one who trusted you and believed in you, and today you have fallen in my eyes too. You did not even once think of my trust in you, you just had to do this."

Yusuf stood there flabbergasted, and began to say, "I don't know what you are talking about."

Baba slapped him very hard and said, "You have already betrayed me, now don't insult my intelligence by denying it. Please leave my home, and never step here again. I have lost a friend today, but you have lost the chance to be a good human being. Trust me, it's a bigger loss for you."

Yusuf walked away quietly. He saw me standing in my doorway, he smiled at me and left. Baba sat in his study till very late afternoon, and I sat in my room weeping. At lunch Baba came out and I served him lunch, he acted as if nothing had happened. When he got up, he looked at me and said, "I want you to understand that this never happened, and that we shall never speak about this to anyone, ever."

Somehow I felt a big distance between Baba and me from that day. He had never said it in so many words, but his behavior had spelt it out that I had betrayed his trust. Baba had closed this chapter of my life, and I had no say in it. I felt like a criminal, and that I should be ashamed of my crimes all my life. There was no need to even talk to me about it; I did not matter, what mattered was what the society would think of it, and what Baba thought was good for me. Even though I knew that he was right, I still felt I should have been given a chance for closure. Someone had cemented that door and I was stuck inside, forever.

Next morning Mamu came to see Baba. He told me Baba had called him over and that there was something they needed to tell me. I felt a little relieved, thinking that maybe now I could speak up, or at least say I'm sorry for my mistakes, and the ice between me and Baba would melt.

I was called into Baba's study. I stood there like a prisoner about to be sentenced, but still hoping for a pardon. Baba asked Mamu to speak to me. Mamu showed me the photo from Shabir uncle's letter. It was a man, simple-looking. Then he said, "We have selected this boy for you, and you are to be married in a month." The marriage was to take place in London, due to visa issues.

Abbas was the name of the man I was to marry. He was a doctor in England, and was about four years older than me. Uncle Shabir had known him for a while, and felt that he would be a perfect match for me.

There it was; my sentence had been passed, I had to pay for my crime, and hence I was in no position to question or negate.

Baba clasped my hands together and embracing them with his own hands, looked into my eyes and said, "This is good for you. Trust me, do this for me and your mom, you will be well taken care of, you will have a respectable life."

I was amazed at Baba's confidence in perceiving my future. He knew and had planned everything to the last Z.

I heard myself saying, "Yes Baba, I will." I knew I could do anything for him.

So Baba had finally realized that he had neglected his duties as a father, and he was correcting it now, thus he was content. Yusuf got a slap on his cheeks, and realized that he had been caught red-handed, and didn't have the courage to face the truth. So he thought, "No fun wasting time here," and he happily moved on to greener pastures.

I, on the other hand had been pushed on to a path that I had to take, and it didn't matter whether my heart was still in shackles – my feet could walk, so I had to move on.

I informed Selma about my marriage proposal, and she was happy for me. I couldn't tell her how attached I was to Yusuf, and I guess it didn't matter what lay hidden in my heart. This was for me to handle alone; it was a crime I had committed in the eye of society. I had decided that since it was my pain and I wasn't allowed to share it with anyone, I did not

UNSPOKEN

need to show my scars to my husband. My life with Abbas would be a new life. My past would be left buried in the sands of time.

Mamu had visited Selma that week, and Selma had informed me that she would not be able to see me off for the wedding. Her father was in bad health. She sent a little wedding gift for me, a box made of walnut wood, beautifully carved, and inside it were amazing colorful glass bangles. Selma knew how we both loved glass bangles, and how for Eid we would spend hours trying to find the perfect match to our dress.

15

Next week Baba and I flew to London, where I was to be married to Abbas. The wedding was a simple affair; it was just Baba and Uncle Shabir from my side. Abbas, on the other hand, had quite a bit of family settled in England. He had two married brothers, one married sister, and a mother. His mother stayed with Abbas since he was the youngest and was not married till now. Shabir uncle was very confident about Abbas being a good match for me. He had told Baba that Abbas was already being funded by the government for research on cancer. He was very brilliant, and had a sparkling future before him. The quality that Shabir liked about him most was that Abbas was a very positive person, so full of energy, always enjoying every bit of his life. Shabir thought that was an aspect which I really needed. He said that Abbas would complete what was lacking in my quiet life.

A week after the wedding, Baba left for home. I was like a lost bird in a cage. Once again Baba assured me that this was best for me.

Baba gave me all of Mom's jewelry and said it was from him. Then he gave me a wooden box like the one Selma had sent for me, and said, "This is from your mom." When I opened the box, it was filled with champa flowers. We hugged each other and cried intensely. Baba cried because he was missing Mom, and I cried because Baba was now physically going away from me. After Baba left I placed both the boxes in a special place in my new closet. Well, everything was new for me: this life, the people around me, and even the place. I literally had to start from scratch.

Like always, I did not argue with life. I just bowed my head and moved ahead. I wonder at and admire people who can take life by its wrist and turn it around. I always thought that was wrong, it was interfering with God's plans, but how do we know what is God's plan? First I had lived the life that Baba had planned for me, except for a detour that lasted for a few months. Now I would be living the life that Abbas was expecting from me. I wonder which one was God's plan.

Well! I think God was watching over all this planning, because Abbas was very nice to me. He adored me, and loved everything I did or said. In a lot of ways he reminded me of Yusuf. I guess Yusuf trampled over my heart first, and destroyed my ability to love anyone the way I had loved him.

I was chiseled very well by the values that mom and Baba had instilled in me, and I became a perfect wife and a perfect daughter-in-law. Everyone around us was surprised by how my mother-in-law doted over me; it was a rare case. In making this bargain I had become everything that everyone expected me to be, but in this race to be accepted, I had lost myself somewhere, lying hidden in the depths of my soul.

However, whenever I had a moment to myself, I would miss Yusuf, and be mad at him for leaving me in the lurch. Sometimes I would walk into the forest behind our house, and in the silence of those woods, I would yell out his name. I always hoped that his voice would echo back, but it never did. There were days when I would think of him so deeply that I was sure he was standing right behind me. My eyes searched for him everywhere. I had still not accepted the fact that Yusuf was a mere shadow, and in the light of life, shadows disappear. I couldn't let go of him. Time was not healing my wound, but was keeping it fresh.

It was a weird time that I was going through; my heart belonged to Yusuf, my body belonged to Abbas, and I was still supposed to be living.

A few weeks after I was married, Abbas took me sightseeing. He wanted me to see how beautiful London was. To him I was a girl from a small village in India, and London was totally a different world. As we walked around Trafalgar square and viewed all the majestic buildings, what amazed me most was Big Ben. I was so excited, and told Abbas that we have a similar tower in Lucknow – it was called the Clock Tower, and it looked exactly like Big Ben. Abbas laughed at me, and said, "There is no comparison," but it made me feel as if I had never left Lucknow, or that Lucknow had followed me. Gradually London began to feel like home.

My husband spent a lot of hours at work on his research, and he would always apologize for not spending enough time with me. But I would always be there, waiting obediently for him whenever he returned home. In about six months, after I had decorated and redecorated the house, I was bored and very alone. I would sit and write long letters to Selma and Baba, and wait for their replies. I was very comfortable, I had no stress, but I had long empty days. I hated this because whenever I was alone, thoughts of Yusuf would come and make me miserable. I couldn't handle the guilt of thinking about him, even after I was married to Abbas. I tried and tried, but like an addiction I couldn't let him go.

Abbas became very successful, and we became very rich. I had a beautiful mansion-like house, with every luxury under the sun, yet nothing could fill that empty spot inside me. I was happy, but I wasn't living. Sometimes I would get so angry at myself over why I could not forget Yusuf, why wasn't he getting out of my heart.

I would remind myself that he wasn't worthy of my love and loyalty, but I would just crumble up. I had read somewhere that if you really love someone, and keep calling out to him, love would answer your call, and it would bring him to you. Every day I kept thinking of him, calling him, I just wanted to see him once, and say my goodbye to him. But he never appeared. I knew my love was true, but I also doubted his love for me; no wonder my calls were coming back empty.

16

It was the third year of our marriage and I was carrying our first child. He was a boy, and we had planned to name him Adil. One day during my eight month, I started getting severe pains. I was rushed to the hospital. Our boy was born, but as a still-born. Abbas was torn apart, he couldn't face me, and he knew that no amount of words could ease the loss of our child.

I felt like a criminal; I had killed a living being. I was so numbed with this pain, I didn't want to come out of it. To make things worse, Abbas had not come to see me in the hospital at all.

One night, two days after my miscarriage, I lay awake, staring at the blank white ceiling of my hospital room. I felt my life, like that white ceiling, was blank and empty. My tears wouldn't stop rolling down my cheeks. I could feel my pillow soaking in them. I lay so weak and helpless, I just wanted someone to hold me and tell me that life would get better. Suddenly I smelt a very familiar fragrance in my room, the smell was so intense that it filled the whole room; even my hands and body recognized it. It was the smell of champa flowers. I started to sob loudly, I got up from my bed and looked all around me in the dark, and yelled, "Mom!" The door opened and I could barely see the shadow of a woman coming close to me. What I saw was a very loving face staring down at me, and caressing my forehead. It was an Indian grief counselor employed by the hospital, who had come to visit me and console me. She was wearing a champa flower in her hair. She had a long chat with me, and I told her about Mom, and the champa. She said she loved the flower too; now that it was available here in the Indian market, she wears one every day. As she was leaving, I asked if she could give me her flower, which she very kindly did. I placed the flower under my pillow, and finally fell into the first deep sleep in three days.

That night I dreamt of a scene that had occurred about few days before I got married and somehow I had pushed it back in to my subconscious. It was a week before we had to leave for London. I was busy getting my last minute shopping done. Yusuf's sting had not left me for a moment, but I had no way of showing my scars to the world. I had just finished my shopping and Mamu stepped out on the street to hail a rickshaw. Suddenly in the midst of all the market place chaos, I heard a laugh which made me turn around in tears. It was Yusuf; he was standing with a group of young girls across the street and having a snack of chaat from the street vendor. All the girls were giggling away as he entertained them. There wasn't a fragment of pain on his face. Life was moving on for him as usual, as if he had taught me the lesson of love, and now he had moved on to teach a million other hopeless hearts. I still felt so hypnotized by him. I walked across to him. He didn't see me, and his group of girlfriends looked at me weirdly as I stared at him. Impulsively, I took his hand, and as though I were under a spell, hypnotized, I said, "How are you?"

He was shocked to see me, he fumbled with some words and then said, "Well, I'm fine, how are you? I heard you are getting married, good for you."

One of the girls dragged him away, saying that they would be late for the movie. Yusuf just walked away, without ever looking back at me or saying goodbye, or "I'm sorry for playing with your heart."

I stood there, shocked; I couldn't understand why I was so hurt. I always knew that our friendship would not be accepted, and that it would have to end one day. But this was too soon.

What shocked me was that Yusuf was so ready for this end. Suddenly I felt I didn't know who this man was. Did I ever know him? I was so hurt by his callousness that I actually felt a few veins rupture inside me and a huge tear form across my heart. I knew this scar was so deep that it would never heal.

When Mamu found me I was shivering vigorously. He held me and took me to the rickshaw. We sat in the rickshaw but my eyes were still following Yusuf, even as we were moving farther and farther away from each other. My heart was still running towards him.

Mamu saw me crying, he lovingly put his hand on my head and said, "You will get over him, trust me, he was never worthy of you." Just then I woke up with those last lines of Mamu still echoing in my mind. It had been four years now and I still wasn't over Yusuf, or should I say I wasn't ready to let go of him. He was still out of my control; he could enter my dreams and my life as he pleased.

My door opened and there in all his humaneness

stood the man that loved me. Abbas had finally found the courage to face me. We hugged each other, as if we were long lost friends.

He kissed me all over my face and said, "I'm here now, we will be fine, I will never leave you alone again."

I wept like a stream on his sturdy shoulders. As Abbas kept consoling me, I realized in this intense moment of pain that Abbas, Baba, Mamu, and Selma were the only people concerned about me. Reality once again stared rudely at my face. Yusuf, the person for whom my heart had ached all these years, for whom I was like a loyal puppy, that man wasn't even aware of my existence. This definitely didn't mean love.

I think I grew up a little that moment, and as people say, everything happens at the right time. It was the right time, for life was about to throw a major curve ball at me.

17

On August 25th, Mamu called to inform us that Baba had had a heart attack, and was in critical condition. I took the earliest flight to Lucknow. Everything, in the name of modernization, had changed so much in Lucknow in these few years. I had lost the place that I once saw as home. I went straight from the airport to the hospital. Baba had just been moved from the ICU to a regular room. We all chatted away with Baba. He was in such a nice mood, very happy to see me. We read some old poems to Baba, and he got all triggered up, and started reciting some new ones to me; it felt like old times.

It was getting late, and the nurse informed us that visiting time was over. Baba asked Mamu to take me home.

As I was leaving, Baba held my hand for the first time and said, "I'm happy you came. I have so much to tell you." He said that the doctor had told him he would be able to go home within couple of days.

On our way home, Mamu told me that it was a close call for Baba, and joked that Baba just wanted to see me. It felt good that Baba might have wanted to see me. I'm sure he was very lonely. Baba's house felt so silent and empty. I asked Mamu to stay with me. That whole night I couldn't sleep. I don't know why, but my heart felt very heavy, as if I couldn't breathe. I kept walking around the house, and each corner, each wall had some memory to narrate to me. Mamu kept chatting with me about his son, Sheraz, who was about six years old now. Mamu was waiting eagerly for the morning, so that he could introduce me to that little baby who had given him so much joy, and who wasn't that little any more. I agreed to go over the next morning to see the joy of Manu's life. Mamu stayed up with me till around 2 am, then finally his tired body gave in and he fell asleep next to me on the sofa. I still couldn't sleep and kept roaming around the empty house.

Around 5 am, the phone rang. It was the hospital, and they informed me that Baba had just passed away. We had not expected this. Baba was supposed to come home in a few days; we had so much to share with each other. But going through life the way I did, surprisingly, I took it bravely. I was amazed that I took Baba's death as another fact of life, death being the only truth in life which no one could evade. Mom's death had shattered me, but I still lived on. I had become more realistic and hence I could face Baba's death so plainly. After all, I had no control over life, so what control could I have over death? I couldn't tell Baba that I was sorry and ashamed that I had broken his faith.

Even at my age, I felt what it was to be an orphan. I felt my childhood had ended and this chapter of my life had concluded.

The funeral arrangements were all made by Mamu. We had informed Selma and her family. Selma's dad was very ill, so Selma came alone with her brother. A lot of people came, and Baba had a very loving and respectful send off. After all, he had never been bad to anyone in his life, and people loved him. Amongst the crowd of loving faces, I saw a boy who might have been about thirteen. He looked very distraught, and was weeping a lot. I went over to Mamu and quietly inquired about this well-wisher of Baba that I didn't know.

Mamu told me that his name was Asif. Some years

ago Baba met him in his courthouse, serving tea to the staff. He was a very cheerful and a smart boy and Baba liked him. When he inquired about him, he learned that Asif was an orphan, and he lived in the orphanage next door. Asif was a boy of great self-pride. He worked to save money so that one day he too could become a lawyer. Baba went over to the school and paid the fees, so that Asif could study. When Asif heard of this, he refused the favor. Baba convinced him that when he became a lawyer, he could return the favor by working free for him. Mamu took me over to Asif, and introduced me to him. He was very polite and humble. He wanted to say a lot, but his tears kept chocking his voice, and excusing himself, he ran out of the house.

All of Baba's friends sat with me, and kept telling me old stories about Baba. They all had such a fondness for him, as if he were the light in their lives and now it had gone. I had never known this side of Baba, and I wished I did.

Shamefully, even in this somber crowd, my eyes still searched for Yusuf. I asked Mamu why he hadn't come. Mamu just shook his head in disgust and said, "I don't think he'll come, you know he never did care for anyone. Baba trusted him too much. He broke his trust and I don't need such a man's prayer for my brother." Mamu looked very apprehensively at me; he had realized that I still wasn't over Yusuf.

After the funeral, Selma said that she couldn't wait any longer, as she had to get back to take care of her dad. I knew she didn't want to go, and I didn't want her to go. We both had so much we wanted and needed to tell each other, but we had to wait for the right time.

As Selma was leaving, she caught my hand very firmly, and sternly looked into my eyes, and said, "What is this about Yusuf? Don't you lie to me, are you a lunatic? You are married now, whatever it was, it happened in another life, let go of it." Again childlike, I listened to Selma's advice, but I knew this time it would be very difficult to do what was expected of me.

My eyes were still waiting to see Yusuf, but he never came. In a week, I settled all the house affairs and left them in Mamu's capable hands, and decided to leave for London.

At the airport, I wanted to cheer Mamu, as I knew I had disappointed him. I told him that I was expecting my second child.

Mamu was so thrilled. He blessed me and said, "I

know it will be an amazing girl like you. You are very precious to me. Don't waste your life, cherish it, it is God's gift to you." I wished Baba could have known about the baby before he left. I thought we would have more time together.

I wanted to hug Mamu, and tell him, "Please forgive me, I am trying really hard to let go of Yusuf," but I couldn't. That door of conversation had been shut on me a long time ago. I was told never to talk about it, as if that would make it disappear. Once again I left India feeling like a criminal, who was sentenced for life. From the plane I looked very nostalgically at the city that lay below, my home and my country. Something scared me inside and was asking me, "Would I ever come back?"

18

Nadia our daughter was born on April 26th. I was the happiest woman; I was blessed with motherhood. When I first held Nadia's little hands in my palm, I thought I had the world in my hands, and that twinkle in her eyes brightened every corner of my life. Abbas was ecstatic, and I felt so content that I was able to give him the happiness he always deserved. I felt guilty at the same time, as to why I couldn't erase Yusuf from my heart. I felt I was cheating Abbas, whom I could never love wholeheartedly, all because of a man who had never loved me! I hated myself.

Nadia was about four months old when Selma called to inform me that her father had passed away. He had killed himself by stepping in front of a moving train. Later Selma learnt from Yaqoob that he had spoken to her father, and told him about his attachment to Selma. Her father was furious and tried to hit Yaqoob, but that spineless creature had threatened to spread the word to everyone in the community about Selma's rape. He said he did not care if he had to go to jail for his crime. Yaqoob had told her father that he wouldn't let Selma get married to anyone else but him. Selma's father knew that once defamed, Selma would never get married. This was a blow that Selma's father couldn't bear. Yaqoob had totally destroyed his daughter. The police couldn't figure out if this was an accident, or if Selma's father intentionally walked in front of a running train. He didn't have a chance to tell anyone this truth, or perhaps he had decided to leave it unspoken.

Selma was in great shock, and she knew that her father had killed himself. She knew that her father could never swallow this truth. No father could ever live with such bitterness. If Yaqoob loved her, as his gang claimed, why would he tell her father this truth? That was enough to prove how selfish and conceited he was. Selma could never forgive him for killing her father. She also told me that, since her father had passed away, they had to move again to live with her step-mom's parents. Selma was absolutely alone and lost. I wished I could be there with her, but Nadia was too little to travel to a foreign land.

I talked to Selma every day till they moved. It became very hard to reach Selma at her step-mom's home. They wouldn't give her the phone. Selma had told me that Yaqoob had followed her even there. I was really worried for Selma.

Selma thought that Yaqoob had gone crazy. He did nothing but follow Selma where ever she went. Selma thought that Yaqoob was trying to cover up his guilt, by showing feelings of compassion for her. He was not capable of a pious emotion called love. I was very suspicious, and I couldn't believe that people like Yaqoob were capable of compassion or conscience. He was a street rat who did not care about what the world said or did to him. I felt this was just another game to entertain his friends. Every Friday Selma would take the subway and go along with her brother to visit her father's grave. Yaqoob knew this and would be there before them, waiting outside the graveyard. Selma couldn't understand – how many other lives did he want to destroy to fulfill his desires?

Whenever I had a chance to connect with Selma, I would spend hours consoling her, telling her to just learn to ignore Yaqoob. But she would always convince me that it was impossible, because he followed her like a shadow and would appear everywhere she went. I could hear in her voice hopelessness, and fear. She told me that now her step-mom was forcing her to get married. She wanted to get rid of her, as soon as possible. After all, her step-mom had no attachment to Selma.

For about four months I didn't hear from Selma. She did not call or write. I felt, in this somewhat small world, that I had lost my dear friend. They say for a woman, half her world is her father and the other half is her husband. After the death of our fathers, both Selma's world and mine had suddenly shrunken, their boundaries smaller.

About six months later, I received a phone call from Mamu that numbed every sense in me, and tears rolled down at the loss of my dearest friend. Selma had hung herself from the ceiling fan of her room one night, and she passed away from this horrible world.

Mamu said that the weirdest thing that happened was this: when he came to Selma's step-mom's home on her request, he found Selma dead. As he entered the house he remembered seeing Yaqoob standing outside. Mamu knew a bit about Yaqoob's harassment. He flew into a rage after seeing Selma and rushed after Yaqoob like a madman, yelling and abusing Yaqoob. Yaqoob looked confused, and as soon as Mamu broke down crying and shouting, "You killed my sweet girl, you bastard!" Yaqoob ran across the street to see what had happened. As soon as he blindly stepped on to the busy street, he was hit by an eight-wheeler and tossed into the air. Only shreds of his body touched the earth again.

This all took place right in front of the home of the person he had proclaimed himself to love. Mamu said that it was the most horrific death anyone could get. Some of Yaqoob's friends came and started yelling, "His love was true, and he gave his life because there was nothing without her in his life."

Mamu said, "It is so crazy that people have started to think that they were true lovers." I was flabbergasted; I put the phone down and sat in my chair with a million absurd thoughts echoing in my heart and mind.

Did he actually love her, was this love? I, who knew all the unspoken truths of Selma's life, thought and believed that this was God's unspoken justice. Then what about me and Yusuf? Was that love? Yaqoob had destroyed Selma and yet he claimed that he loved her. Yusuf had destroyed my heart, yet I claimed that it was love. Maybe I was wrong. Like every human, Yaqoob too may have been capable of loving.

There was a letter that they found in Selma's cold hands. It read, "I forgive everyone and hold no one responsible for my pain or death. I forgive the gravest sins done to me, in this hope, that God may forgive my sin of taking my own life."

Selma and I had been away from each other so long, yet I never felt we were apart. Her death had made my world so empty that, alas, I was left friendless.

Mamu's words kept ringing in my ears. He was getting suspicious that maybe Selma had loved Yaqoob, and hence her father killed himself. He thought that maybe Selma's father should have agreed, maybe we could set up Yaqoob with some business and all would be well. Mamu was a noble soul who hadn't seen the harsh side of life, and so he believed that people could change for the better. I thought it was because of his compassionate heart that he had also easily forgiven me. I wished I could tell Mamu the truth. Only I knew Selma's truth, but it was too late, so late that the truth had to be kept silent.

The last few months had taught me unforgettable life lessons about friendship and love. I knew Selma had forgiven me, but I could never forgive myself. Selma's death had made it very difficult for me to forget this guilt, that I too was responsible for her untimely demise. I was starting to realize that if we had not remained silent after our clash with Yaqoob, we could have saved Selma and her father's life. But in a society where girls are groomed to keep such incidents unspoken, unfortunately it is they alone who pay the price for remaining unspoken.

About a month after Selma's death, I received a letter from her. She had mailed it a day before her death. The letter read:

Dear Sharmeen,

I know I have not written or spoken to you for quite a while. I feel every time I call you or write to you, I just overwhelm you with my problems. This is my last letter to you. I too have gotten too fed up with the misfortunes of my life. Yesterday Yaqoob came over, and said that he needed to talk to my step-mom. She was right there and she willingly invited him in. I didn't know this, but he had been previously meeting with her. Somehow Yaqoob had convinced my step-mom that he was really interested in marrying me, and would keep me very happy. The devil must have been very kind to him, because he had started a small grocery store and it was doing pretty well. My step-mom would go and get a lot of free stuff from Yaqoob. I was so ashamed to learn of this, and today he had come to finalize the date of his marriage to me.

My step-mom stared at me and said, "Be happy that someone wants to marry you, you are not some princess."

I couldn't believe what was happening. Yaqoob handed me some flowers that he had brought for me, and I flung them in his face. I knew that I had to take matters into my hands; after all it was my life. How could I ever marry the man who had raped me, and killed my father?

My dear friend, I have but one choice. If I cannot live a decent life, then I don't need to live. Please forgive me, I intentionally didn't share this with you, because I knew you would stop me, but it's time for me to depart from this brutally distorted world.

Be of good cheer and remember me always, as your truest friend.

Be brave, be strong, and know that I will always be with you.

Goodbye

Selma

19

The pain of Selma not being there had distorted my world. However, Nadia's innocent face kept me moving on with life. I never told Abbas the actual circumstances of Selma's death. He was only told that she was my best friend, and that she died in a horrible accident. Once again I wanted to just let go of everything, especially myself, and fall apart. But Nadia's little hands caressing my face could wipe off even the deepest scars of sorrow. Every so often, I would pick up the phone to call Selma, wanting to share a newly given joy from Nadia. It would take several minutes, and pointless dialing of the unforgettable number, for reality to jolt my nerves and remind me that Selma was no more.

When Mom passed away, I had Selma to hold me; even when Baba passed away, she was there. She was my crutch. I hadn't learned to walk without her.

Suddenly I looked behind, and there was only emptiness, as if someone was gradually erasing everything that I held dear.

A few weeks later, Abbas's mother passed away. It was a very big setback for him. I felt as if someone had cursed me. What was happening? Like a deck of cards, my life was crumbling.

I would watch Abbas mourn silently in his study in the evenings. He seemed so devastated that he hardly played with Nadia. I couldn't understand why it had hit him so hard. His mother was eighty-two years old, and had been in bad health for a while. She had had a very full life in which all her kids loved her and took very good care of her. They all knew that she would go any day.

Abbas had started to worry me. He had stopped eating well, and if I forced him, he would throw up. One day as I went into his study to give his evening tea, I saw him weeping. I melted like a candle at his feet, and pleaded with him to tell me what was wrong. He cupped my face in those warm hands of his, and said, "I have been hiding something from you and it's time that I tell you."

I sat upon the chair next to him, and he kept holding my hands to his face as he spoke.

"You have been the love of my life, you have been a wonderful wife to me and the best friend I could ever have. This has made it more difficult for me to leave this world, because I don't want to leave you." My heart began to race, leave me? Why would he have to do that? Then he said the words that I never wanted to hear.

"I have been diagnosed with pancreatic cancer. This is God's will, and even I, a cancer specialist, did not see this coming. My time is up, I have but a few months left. I am taking some chemo now, so that I can finish some of the things I need to take care of." I sat there frozen, while he kept talking, as if there was really very little time left.

As he described how he had made our future secure, my mind kept drifting back to when I had just married him, and how I was so unsure of a person who was such a stranger to me. How he had given me time to fall in love with him, never forcing or taking advantage of being my husband. We first became good friends and then lovers and now parents. I had grown so much with him. He had taught me so much about life, and love. Now he, too, was leaving me.

He shook me and said, "Did you listen to what I

said? It is all very important, you guys will be fine."

I couldn't understand why life was being so cruel to me. I held his hands over my face and bitterly cried, "I wouldn't have the warmth of these hands around me, and it is their warmth that makes me feel that I exist. Please don't go. O my God, let him live for me at least."

I started to go with him for his chemotherapy sessions. The hospital was right in the center of the busy city. Abbas hated the noise and pollution. He had spent half his life closed up in research labs, and in the quiet sanctuary of our home in the suburbs. Noise and crowds made him very anxious. We would never take Nadia to the hospital, because I didn't want her to see her father suffer or to see even a glimpse of the upcoming catastrophe.

I had a very good neighbor, who was originally from China. We had hardly spoken to each other over the years, but we acknowledged each other's existence. Her daughter was five years older than Nadia, so she would always watch out for Nadia in the school bus. Shirley was my neighbor's name and her husband's name was Chan. Shirley had lost her brother to cancer few years ago. Even though we were just neighbors, pain and loss had suddenly made us closer. Once every three weeks when we needed to go to the hospital, we would leave Nadia with Shirley. On our way back we would stop and buy some candy or treats for Nadia, and Abbas always insisted on buying flowers for me. He knew how much I loved flowers. I would always tell everyone that no matter how sad I am, flowers can always cheer me up. Their beauty would assure me that the world is still beautiful and life is worth living.

Abbas's last few days were very horrible. I couldn't bear to see him suffer the way the disease and its treatment had burnt him. We spent a lot of quality time together. We never spoke about his going, but every day we celebrated his being with us. There were people always around him, and Nadia was the light in his life's flickering candle. Sometimes, when we were alone and he would get all emotional with me about how much he loved me and how he didn't want to leave me, I would see Nadia standing in the corner of the room and looking at her father with yearning eyes.

It reminded me of when Baba doted over Mom and I would feel left out. I called Nadia and made her sit next to her father, and I told her that she was the joy of our life. Abbas would hug her, and whisper his sweet nothings into her ears and peer at me over her shoulders. I wanted Nadia to get all of her father's love, which I never got. From my own life's experience I understood very well that for a daughter, a father is her own shining star that lights her entire world. He is the first man in her life, who will shape her outlook towards other men. She will see the world through his eyes, and will hold his little finger for support, all her life. I took a lot of videos of Abbas. I wanted to capture every moment of his life and his presence for Nadia's future.

Nadia was taking ballet classes in school. It was her performance day, she so wanted her dad to come and see her, but Abbas by now had become bedridden. I had asked one of my friends to videotape the show. That night Nadia was excited that her dad would be able to finally see her, in all her charm and glory.

We had dinner and I told Nadia that once I had finished my kitchen chores, we would all sit together and watch her video. We had rented a hospital bed and placed it in our family room, so Abbas could be there and watch TV too.

When I was nearly done with my work, I called Nadia and told her to take a glass of water and place it next to her dad's bed, and that I'd be right there to start the video. After giving Abbas the water, Nadia came back very upset. She said, "Mom, Dad's gone to sleep, and I think he doesn't want to watch me dance." It was only 7:30 pm. I looked at the clock and thought it was too early for him to fall asleep. Before I could complete my thought I ran into the family room. Abbas was lying on his side, his eyes were shut tight. I called out to him. I was so scared to go near him. It took a lot of courage to cover those few steps to his bedside. I held his hand, and those hands that had warmed me with love for years were ice cold now. I fell flop on the ground near his bed. Somewhere in the corner of my heart, I was living with this fiction that he would never die, and that we would continue living like this, in his presence.

I kept rubbing his hands on my face and breathing in them, hoping foolishly to transfer the warmth of my life into him. Abbas had quietly slipped away from us, and no matter what I did, he wouldn't come back. I kept holding his hand, and I wept like I had never wept before. The man who had loved me was no more. I had never felt more alone in my life. The tree that shaded me from every harsh wind of life had died, and I was left without even his shadow.

Uncle Shabir took care of the funeral arrangements. After Abbas was buried, I felt as if my whole life till then was buried with him. I felt as if someone had buried my heart with him, it had become so difficult to even breathe. Abbas was buried in a small cemetery in the countryside, which was shared by people of different faith. Abbas didn't want to be buried in the Muslim cemetery in the city. I remembered on one of our trips to the city, after Nadia was born, Abbas expressed how he hated this noise and pollution of the city. He had commented that he wouldn't want to be caught dead here. That's when he had expressed his desire to be buried in this cemetery, way out in the countryside.

We would often drive past this cemetery, and Abbas would always say, "I wouldn't mind spending my afterlife here." It was really very serene and beautiful.

I had to once again begin life anew. I sold the house and we moved to a less expensive area, near the airport. Now that Abbas wasn't there, it did not matter where we lived. I bought a small condo; after all, it was just Nadia and me now. I wanted to save all the capital that Abbas had left us for Nadia's studies and her wedding.

I had lived my life, and did not need much, but it was a big change for Nadia. She had become used to living in a big mansion, and being treated like a princess. Life was going to teach her many new lessons, and I was getting her ready for them. The first thing we did in the new condo was put up Abbas's photos everywhere; I never wanted Nadia to forget her father. I included a very lively picture of him playing with Nadia; she needed to know this that her father loved her immensely.

We often forget to tell our children how much we love them. We assume they know, but they always need to see it in action, too. Love is too intense a feeling to be expressed only in words. Love needs to be demonstrated, at every age, and at every level of our life.

Sometimes after I dropped Nadia at school, I would drive back to our old house where there was a new family living now. I could imagine that this house was witnessing a new story. If walls could narrate, they would tell us the most amazing things.

I would look at the cherry blossom tree that Abbas and I had planted in our front yard, which was still covered with flowers. Once I remember Abbas and I had gone on a hiking trip. After walking up the mountain for about two hours, we were completely exhausted. We sat down on the bare ground, surrounded by a lot of trees, including some fallen ones. Abbas was quite a nature freak. He showed me this huge tree trunk that had been cut down. There were a million minute circles, running from the center of the cut trunk to its outer edge. Abbas said, "Do you know, each circle represent each year this tree has lived? If one counts them, we can know how old this tree was." He began examining it in more detail, and I began to think of the life that this tree had witnessed. After all, its script was also written down by nature. I lay my hand softly on the trunk, and closed my eyes. It was so silent in the forest that I thought I could actually feel the tree talk to me, or maybe it did. Every piece of dirt, dust, rock, and trees, has a story to tell, if only they could speak, or if we knew how to listen to them.

I had become exhausted trying to begin life from scratch again and again. Sometimes I just didn't feel like moving another step. I knew I still had to live for two reasons; one was because Nadia needed me, and the other being that life was not ready to end yet.

I had become very lonely. I felt that I had walked this long road, and on each corner one loved one left my hand, and today without Baba, Selma, Adil (our lost son), and now with Abbas gone, I was left all alone with only Nadia still holding my hand. I never wanted to leave her alone, but I knew when my time was up, one day I would have to leave too.

City life was very chaotic. The apartments were very small, and the area very noisy as well as not so clean. There were lots of Asians living in this neighborhood. They were all from a lower income strata, but were very closely knit and caring. Nadia started to make friends easily, but I didn't like the schools. At night there was crime on the streets, the noise of screams and police cars zooming by. All this would scare Nadia and even me. Nearly every night, she would come running to my room scared. That's when I started this ritual of taking her away from the gory reality to a place of angels and fairies. I started telling her bedtime stories. When you tell stories to a child, you run through the whole encyclopedia of fairy tales a bit too soon. That's when I started to use my old skill of writing. I had always loved to write, but never had the time or the inspiration. It felt nice writing children's stories. I realized I was pretty spontaneous, as if I had tons of them just waiting to be poured out. Nadia loved my stories, but her only demand was that each story had to end in a happy way. She said she hated sad endings, and I needed to heal that wound which was making her feel this way.

No matter how much I tried to shelter her, Nadia, like her father, hated the city atmosphere all around us. I spoke to Uncle Shabir, and he advised me that living in the city with a young kid was a bad idea. He said his son, who was a real estate agent, would look for a small house in his area. I thought it was best that we stayed near Uncle Shabir, to have at least some manly support in our lives. After about a six-month search, we found a house about six blocks from Uncle Shabir. The family that lived there was going through a rough divorce, and was in a rush to sell the house and split. We got the house for half the price, since I paid full in cash. It was a very sweet small house, country cottage-style. Above all, it also had a good enough backyard, where Nadia could play. Nadia was already about eleven years old. We admitted her to a good school there. I loved the house, but I still was very uneasy spending the money that Abbas had left for us. I felt only Nadia should have it.

I took up a part time job at the public library. It felt nice being among people, and that way I didn't have to keep staring at the emptiness of my life. Nadia kept me quite preoccupied, too.

As she grew, her life kept getting more and more

busy and so did mine; after all, my life was for her. Nadia became a very studious and quiet child. She mainly kept to herself. We hardly ever spoke about Abbas. I felt she might be feeling betrayed, that her dad shouldn't have left her. Sometimes when I walked into her room with a cup of milk, I would see her staring at the picture of her with her dad. As soon as she saw me, she would look the other way.

I know how tough it was for her, and I wished I could find a way to her heart and heal it. I prayed and prayed that she should have all the courage she needs, that she should have all the happiness she deserves, and that she should have a loving and amazing husband like her dad was to me. Sometimes all one can do, and should do, is pray.

Mamu was my only connection to India now. I would talk to him every week, and he kept insisting that I should come and sell Baba's house, because he was getting too old to take care of it. I was scared to go to India. I was scared of meeting Yusuf.

He still haunted me, I was afraid to face him. I felt he would destroy me again.

Yet every day I would find something that would remind me of him. I would write huge letters to him, writing all the things I never got to tell him and the biggest truth that had been left unspoken: that I loved him immensely. All these untold words had become so toxic over the years that they had begun to eat the insides of my soul. I felt that he should know that there is someone in this world who has honestly and selflessly loved him for the last twenty-five years.

But I think God was intentionally keeping me away from Yusuf. He had played his role in my life and now there would be no reappearances. I never mailed the letters, but just tore them up; it felt good, and it was a kind of therapy, to get out the acid which was corroding my heart...

Life never gave me a chance to fall apart. Every time a calamity occurred, before I could wipe my tears, I had to wipe another's first. When Mom died, I had to take care of Baba; when Baba died I had Abbas and Nadia; now when Abbas departed, I had Nadia in my arms. My only support was Selma, and she too had found an escape.

I am not complaining about my life. God had blessed me with good parents, good friends, a good husband, and an adorable child, but I was always at an edge, fearing which loved one I would lose next. I had become too dreary to love anyone.

It frightened me that I might lose them too.

Even though Nadia avoided talking about her father, I would find ways of narrating stories of his past. How he came from a poor family in India, studied hard, and got a scholarship to come to England. He was an amazing human being who took great care of his family. We would shuffle through his photos, and each picture had a story connected to it. Eventually these became Nadia's bedtime stories, and the ice that had built up melted away into love for her father.

It is surprising that Nadia never asked me about my past; neither did Abbas, and I never said anything.

Sometimes I felt, "I am her mother, she should know about me," but I never gave too much value to myself. I was an ordinary person, with an ordinary life. I never wanted to impose my views, or circumstances of life, on her. I wanted her to form her own opinion about everything. Just because my life had been tough didn't mean her life would be, too. So I kept quiet, and I left her free, without chaining her to my experiences. I wanted her to feel and know life as being good, positive, and spectacular. Her canvas was blank – why should I ask her to paint it with my colors?

Nadia became much braver than me. She was daring, outspoken, and she felt that she deserved good things because she was special. After her graduation, she wanted to go to Egypt to study archeology, under the famous Professor Hamid Khan. I didn't stop her, even though if I could I would follow her to the end of the earth. I had to let her go, so that she could really live her life, and form her own experiences. God willing they would all be good and enriching.

Once Nadia left for Egypt, I suddenly had so much time to myself. It was a weird feeling. I remember I would always say, "One day when I am done with all my duties, I'll do something for myself. I'll live my life." I always loved to write, from the time I was an adult, spontaneous ideas and thoughts would spring to me at odd places and times, and words, lines, scenes would sprout one after the other. Sometimes I would write pages in my dream, and by morning half of it would fade away. It felt weird to get up in the middle of the night and start writing. Abbas would have thought I was crazy. I had my chores and schedule to take care of. I couldn't, like some people, stay up late, and then wake up late, that would disturb everyone else's life.

Now I think maybe I should have tried. I'm sure

something could have been worked out, but I guess my feelings, my wants were never of importance, even to me. I also loved music, and always dreamt of learning how to play the sitar. I remember when Nadia was around twelve I tried to take some classes with an Indian lady in our neighborhood. As usual, my class time began to interfere with Nadia's growing schedule of activities, so I gave up on the sitar.

I had everything I wanted or needed in material things. I had the best of everything. Yet I would often sit and search for myself in this web we call reality. Where was that girl who loved to swing on swings hanging from Banyan trees, where was the girl who ate those crazy sandwiches, who loved those amazingly beautiful glass bangles? Back then even their jingle would send raptures of joy through my heart. Sometimes I would drift into those wondrous days of my youth. I hadn't worn glass bangles for years. I remembered how on every Eid, Selma and I would go with Mamu to the market the night before, to buy our matching sandals and bangles for our Eid outfit.

It was the last Eid before I got married, and that was the last time I bought these bangles. That year, instead of Mamu, Yusuf took us shopping. Baba gave us permission to go with him. Baba and no one else was aware of my attachment to Yusuf at that time. It was a trip I shall never forget. That night Mamu had the flu, and so he asked Yusuf to take his nieces, me, and Selma for our shopping. Yusuf had an old Fiat car in which we had to really pack ourselves. I let one of Mamu's nieces sit in the front with Yusuf, just to tease him. He was pretty irritated. As soon as we reached the main bazaar, Selma caught hold of my arm and dragged me towards shoe stores. She had to have exact matching shoes for her dress. The shoes had to be perfect, good, and cheap. I on the other hand just picked what I liked, without ever seeing the price. Selma would then start her lecture on economical living and how spendthrift and unworldly I was. Thanks to Baba, I never had to compromise my desires for the sake of money. After Selma had spent hours roaming from one store to another, and argued and fought with half of them, I would quietly intervene and add some money and buy the shoes for her. She would complain about it all the way till the bangle store, and then all the colors and glitter would make her forget everything.

Yusuf's eyes were following me everywhere; he was bugged that I wasn't giving him attention. After all, he was doing all this only for me. At the bangle store Yusuf started buying bangles for the other girls, laughing and indulging in light-hearted flirting. Now I began to get edgy. I didn't buy any bangles for myself. Selma had found her pair, and she started to pressure me to get mine, too. Selma by now was very hungry. The whole market was infused with the smell of kabobs, and delicious delicacies, which were a prime sell on this big night.

There were benches laid out all around, and each vendor would serve you freshly cooked food, right there on the street. By now everyone was hungry and they all came and sat next to us at our table. We had already ordered, and Yusuf began to order for everyone else. I felt like tearing the hair from all their heads. All of Mamu's nieces were so childish, giggly, and so like putty in Yusuf's experienced hands. Selma noticed that I was bugged, and was not eating my favorite dishes. She nudged me so hard that my plate fell to the ground. Yusuf right away got up, picked up my mess, and ordered more food for me. I was so mad at him by now, especially by the fact that he had gone and thoughtfully matched and bought bangles for each girl, except me. I didn't care, I didn't want any bangles, and it wouldn't kill me if I didn't have any new ones this year. I pushed my plate away, behaving very childishly, and walked away saying I wasn't hungry any more. This made Selma very mad. She caught my hand, and whispered very curtly, "Sit down, don't be such a baby. You are making a fool of yourself." Those words shook me up; I looked at Selma and her eyes were telling me that she knew what I was up to. I began eating my food, Selma kept staring at Yusuf, and I thought she was going to push him onto the barbecue.

Somehow on the ride back Yusuf manipulated the situation in such a way that I ended sitting in the front seat with him. We stopped by each girl's house and dropped them off one by one. I realized that he was routing the drive in such a way that I would be dropped off last. I was feeling very awkward. When Selma got dropped off, she stared into my eyes and smiled, like a mother saying goodbye to her daughter on her first date, but her eyes were saying much more than her faint smile. I was very nervous. I knew I had made it very obvious to Yusuf that I was affected by his lack of attention. He stopped the car a few blocks before my house. I wanted to spend time with him, and at the same time I wanted to run away from his car. I was too embarrassed, as if I had just confessed to him how crazy I was about him.

The heat in the car was turning to steam. I was sweating, and Yusuf was as cool as an iceberg. He closed in and caught my hand. He then dug through his pocket and took out a bunch of the most beautiful bangles, and slipped them, one by one, onto my wrist. I was speechless, but relieved.

He said, "I haven't seen your new dress, and I don't know whether they will match. I was actually only thinking of you, and every color reminded me of you." He then recited a new couplet that he had just composed at the market place, something to the effect that I was the rainbow of life, and every color had originated from me.

I was mesmerized, just as I think any twenty-one-year-old would have been. Then he kissed both my hands, jingling the glass bangles on them, and said, "This is music to my heart."

I don't know what happened to me; I caught Yusuf's hand tightly. He smiled and asked what I was thinking. I told him that I was trying to create a memory of his hands, so that when he was not around I would remember this touch. It is surprising that Yusuf never asked me to ever marry him, and I never told him that if he did ask, I would shut my eyes and walk anywhere with him. Today I thank God, because I knew that God was looking after me and didn't let me commit the biggest folly of my life. I reminisce today and think it is true that sometimes some things are best left Unspoken.

When I entered my home, I knew then that I had lost my heart forever. I was so happy, yet I kept feeling I had committed a crime. The memory of his hands still lingers, but it gives me only sweet bitterness.

Even when Abbas was alive, whenever I was alone, thoughts of Yusuf would come storming and I would just surrender. At first I had tried to fight with them, because I felt that it was wrong to think of another man, but the more I resisted the more anxious it would make me. After all, I had no control over my dreams and thoughts. Sometimes I would walk into an empty room and yell out his name then burst out crying. Often I would complain: why he couldn't leave me alone, why does he torture me this way? Somebody once told me that we grow up to find answers to our questions. At the age of fifty I realized that Yusuf had not caged me, I had caged him in my heart. It was time to let him go forever. All my life I wanted him, and even after I got married I ran after him, but I never even got a glimpse of him. I was too tired, but wise now. I had to stop running after shadows, and stop hurting myself. I myself was the reason of all this agony in my life. Yusuf wasn't even aware of my existence. Maybe the stories that I had heard of true love were just stories, for he never heard my cries.

After so many years, my mind was free now. I decided that I should start writing. The only topic that I felt passionately about was my best friend Selma. Once I started to write, I realized there was so much that I did not know about Selma, especially her early childhood; and she having had such a brief life span, there wasn't going to be enough material for a book.

It dawned on me that the only person I really knew was I – my own life story.

Mine was an ordinary story, a plain life; why would I write it? I knew that there was no one who really knew me, but did I want to simply pass through this world as an invisible soul? No matter how insignificant I was and how inconsequential my life had been, yet it was the story of a human being, someone who had shared this world with millions of others. I was sure that amongst thousands of books that line the library shelves, mine would be just another book, just another untold story.

Yet a story that, would be unique and different from any other. I would write this book for my daughter, and give it to her at the right time.

But before I could start to write, there were these guilt-pangs that I needed to calm. I knew then that I had to do something meaningful to keep Selma alive. I had this silly notion that I had somehow killed her, and I had to bring her back to life for my own sanity. I never understood that I wasn't God: neither could I kill someone, nor could I bring them back. But something had to be done to make Selma's soul feel good; after all I loved her so. My book had to wait.

This was my new project and it was really driving me insane. I had thought of many projects to help the poor, the blind and deaf, and many of Abbas's rich doctor friends were very willing to fund these projects. But something felt missing; it wasn't special, like Selma. One night, battling with a thousand ideas, I stayed up till 2 am. I was about to call it a night, when the phone rang, and it was Mamu. He sounded very frail. He told me that he was very ill, and that I needed to come to India to sell Baba's house, because he was in no condition to take care of it anymore.

20

The journey back was such a blink that before I knew it I was standing at the gate of Lucknow airport. Sheraz, Manu's son, had come to receive me; he was all grown up, and handsome, too. On our way home, Sheraz told me that Mamu was in the last stages of TB. He had known for a while, but did not mention it to anyone.

We went straight to Mamu's home. He looked so old and weak, and I never wanted to see him so frail. He had always given me, and lot of others, faith and strength. He was among the few good human beings that I had known in my life. I told Sheraz that we should move him to a hospital, it would make him comfortable. Mamu refused, saying, "I don't have the strength to argue with you guys, just let me be in my own home." He said that he knew his time was near, and thus he had called me, to hand over the responsibilities of Baba's property to me.

Mamu had no one else except his son Sheraz, who was only nineteen and was still a student. I consoled Mamu, saying that I was going to take care of him, and that he needn't worry about anything, but just enjoy whatever time was left for him.

In a way I was happy that God had given me this chance to serve Mamu. I knew he loved me as his own daughter. He and Baba would often fight, and they would say that they should have exchanged kids. Mamu always wanted a daughter, and Baba a son. Mamu's wife had passed away from hepatitis when Sheraz was just twelve.

Sheraz and I planned a lot of outdoor activities, so that Mamu could get fresh air. We would take him to his favorite parks, where he and Baba used to walk for hours. Mamu would lie down on his new folding lounge chair in the park, and Sheraz and I would keep chatting with him about Mamu's old time favorite stories. I got to know so much about Baba and Mom from Mamu. It was real quality time.

Then the matter of Baba's house had to be settled. Mamu felt that he wanted it to be settled in front of him, while he was still here. Sheraz found a real estate agent. Many offers came for the house, which was in a very prime location. Once Mamu even suggested to me that I did not have to sell the house, and I should come and settle back here in India. Baba had worked very hard for this house; it had a lot of memories.

Memories, that's what I feared. The real people were no longer there, and memories only hurt. For me this house spoke of past history, but it was time to make some new history. I wasn't too eager to sell the house, but I didn't have any options. I definitely didn't want to stay in India, it would be too painful.

After Friday prayers that week, Mamu passed away, but it was the end of a beautiful life, I knew he would be missed. Very few people came for the funeral, because Mamu didn't make many friends. My family and Selma's family would keep him busy all the time. Mamu's house looked so lonely and eerie without him. I had always loved this house; it reminded me of love and comfort. I walked down to the basement. In Lucknow, basements, which were called *taikhana*, were very common in every house, but somehow there wasn't one in my home. Basements were cold; for the really hot summers in Lucknow, it was a needed luxury.

We were around eleven years old, Selma and me, when it had been decided by Mamu, that every Friday, after school, Baban would drop us at Mamu's house. Baba would come late on Fridays, and Mom would go visiting her friends after Friday prayers. Selma and I, we both loved this plan. Mamu would excitedly wait for this day too. He was an amazing cook, and on hot summer days he would make *gulguley* – sweet flour balls – made with flour, brown sugar, and milk, then fried. When we came back from school, like two warriors, Mamu would take us down to the cool basement and treat us to hot gulguley, topped with vanilla ice cream. Later I realized that this is what people label as comfort food. Oh! It would really soothe our tired souls, and bring smiles on those heat-battered dry lips.

The basement had small windows near the ceiling that looked out at street level. Selma and I would often climb over stored beddings and pillows to get to the window, and look outside. All we could see was people walking by, and we could see only their shoes and feet. As I was wiping that window, it brought back a vision from those past days. There were serious Shia and Sunni riots going on in those days. There was a strict curfew after 8 pm. On Fridays, Selma and I would sleep over at Mamu's house. On one such day, riots erupted suddenly.

We could hear chaos, screams and shouting. Mamu's wife Nabila would be terrified. She always made the scene seem so much tenser. Mamu, on the other hand, would take us down to the basement. This time he had made hot pakoras, and Nabila's famous mint and raw mango chutney. Nabila would refuse to do anything but pray loudly and hide behind the heap of beddings. No matter what Mamu did to make us feel safe and happy, as soon as we could see people running and falling, through that small window, our hearts would sink with fear.

I remember, once I was looking out during these troubled times and I saw a young boy, or at least from his small feet that's what I assumed he was. He was dragging a sword, and it made a horrible sound scraping the concrete ground. He stopped right in front of our window, and sat down on the street. Now that I could see him, he might have been around sixteen years old, his face was covered with blood and sweat, and his white clothes were dirty and torn. He looked exhausted and lost. I was happy that he didn't see me. Suddenly, at that very thought, he turned around and looked straight at me very perversely. Mamu grabbed me from behind and pulled the curtain on the window. To this day, I have not forgotten that boy's face.

I keep thinking, "What is that I saw through that window? terror, bravery, or the beginning of human degeneration?"

This question has haunted me over the years. Why did that boy have to do that, why did anyone have to raise a sword against another human being? My immature mind was convinced that we were born to live with each other, and share this earth, not kill each other. Why was this happening? Why couldn't we just live in peace?

I shook my head to dispel that horrible thought. I didn't want to think of those harsh times anymore. Mamu had given me so much love and care, and taught me lessons of being a good human being and that was all I wanted to remember.

It is strange – why do we only think about the goodness of people after they die? Mamu was like a father to me, a father figure that I had dreamt of having.

I will miss him all my life, but I felt so blessed that he had been a part of my life.

Sheraz was very uncomfortable about living in his house alone. I told him that he needn't worry. I'd go back and sponsor him, and he could live with me in London. He was very upset with Yusuf. He had heard from some friends that Yusuf had returned and was in the city with friends, but he hadn't come to see him.

I just smirked and I rubbed his shoulder and said, "You shouldn't worry about people who don't care for you. Trust me, it's a colossal waste of time, and time is very precious."

Mamu had done a lot for Yusuf's family. When Yusuf's mother was ill, and Yusuf was travelling everywhere for the poetry recitation programs which had become his only source of income, Mamu would take care of his mother. Every day Sheraz would buy her groceries and pay the utility bills, and Mamu would fix things for her. Yusuf was always quite callous. I guess most creative people are. Yusuf didn't even come for Mamu's funeral. Somehow I knew that even if Yusuf was around, he would not have come.

This awareness made me completely detach my heart from him – that which I couldn't do for the last twenty-five years just happened in a split second. My mind for the first time was so clear. I had set him and my heart free. I could love a man who was callous, a flirt, but I could not love a man who wasn't even humane.

We were informed that Yusuf was back in town after two days, but he never visited Sheraz or me to offer condolence. He had this philosophical excuse to avoid life's mundane facts: "When a person is dead, why should we mourn for him?" He never attended funerals, because he thought people just acted out emotions, and there was never a genuine tear. I never agreed with him. I knew even then that he was too afraid to face facts of life, death being the scariest one of all.

I had accepted an offer on the house. I wanted to go back home as soon as possible. I had sent in sponsorship papers for Sheraz to come and settle in London with me. The next morning I was waiting for the buyer as we had to sign some final papers. I wanted to sell Baba's house as is. I didn't have the heart to sell it piece by piece, furniture and other stuff. Looking now at each piece, I could see that although I had grown up, I could still see my innocence and heart scattered all around this house.

I fondly touched each memory and bid it farewell, this part of my life was now over. I would never have to come back here. I could finally leave my pain behind me.

This would be my last day in Lucknow, as after

Mamu's death there was nothing left in India for me. I decided to take one final walk, down those lanes that were edged so vividly into my memory.

I said goodbye to every tree, to each stone that had marked my path for so many years. Every house seemed to speak to me and say their goodbyes.

Then I arrived at Selma's house and my feet stopped.

I saw that huge lock on the gate, and as I peered over it, the lawn seemed too unkempt and mournful. The house and every wall, that had stood witness to a thousand laughs, giggles, screams of joy, cries of pain, whispers of hopes, dreams, fears, now stood so silent. But they all spoke to me many stories of two best friends. Only I could read and hear those whispers. I looked carefully again at that rusted lock. This gate had been closed for a while, the scene had changed, the actors had played their role, and the stage was now quiet.

Even when I passed Yusuf's house, the same scene of loneliness, and emptiness lingered. This door was locked and closed too. Life had moved on, it was I who was still standing there like a fool. I wiped my tears, knowing that they were not mere tears, but pages of my life that I was erasing.

21

When I reached Baba's house, I saw a little girl dressed in printed white cotton fabric, sitting on our front door steps. She was drenched in sweat, and her tears had dried on her face. As I looked at her, she looked straight into my eyes.

Her eyes looked as mysterious as glass marbles. Those eyes could make anyone melt. She looked very fearfully at me and said, "Sorry madam, I was tired so I sat on your steps."

As she got up and walked past me, I spontaneously took her little hand, and said, "That's okay, you can sit and rest." She kind of flopped back on the cement steps, she began to swoon. I ran in and got some water and splashed it on her face; she in turn feebly grabbed the glass from my hand and began to gulp down the water.

I went in and got her some cookies, and she ate

them feverishly fast. I asked her what had happened. She lamented that she lived across that railway line, in a small hut with her parents. Her parents would cross the railway line every morning and go to the town to beg for alms. This morning as they were crossing the line, they were hit by a train and both of them died on the spot. The hut belonged to the local landowner, who had thrown this little girl out. She said she was only nine, she didn't know where to go, or what to do. She had been walking all morning asking people to help her, and everyone told her to just go back home.

Her parents lay there on the tracks for hours, their bodies shattered into pieces. She told me that the railway officers told her that it was too big a mess, so she helped them collect bits of her parents, so they could have something that would stand for a human body, and burial could be done. She didn't have money to bury them.

They were lying in an empty rice sack at the police station. I couldn't move after hearing this ghastly tale. It was difficult to even imagine what this child must have gone through. I ran into the house and threw up, I was sick to my stomach.

No one could have survived this horror. I guess

it was her innocence that was protecting her from the detrimental effect which it could have had on her mind. I don't know from where this rush of courage and rage came into me. I came back out of the house, caught hold of her hand, and led her to the police station. There, I was assured of the truth of this horrific incident. I paid the dues, and we went to the graveyard and had the bodies buried.

When we returned home, the house buyer was waiting there with Sheraz. I had begun to go over the final property papers quickly, as I had a flight to catch. Sheraz was playing with the little girl. I could hear her giggling as he tickled her, and he asked her what her name was.

She sweetly cried, "Selma." My hand stopped. I turned away from the papers, and looked at this little innocent girl, who called herself Selma. I ran and scooped her in my arms. When I hugged her it felt as if I had found the peace that I was looking for. I went up to the buyer, handed the unsigned papers back to him, and I deeply apologized to him, for I had just decided not to sell the house.

After a great deal of grumbling and many more apologies from Sheraz, the would-be buyer left. Then Sheraz looked inquiringly at me, "Why you don't want to sell?" I told Sheraz that this house was going to be a shelter home for this little Selma, and maybe many more destitute and lost souls like her.

As I said those words there was an intense rush of adrenaline through my whole body. I felt as if I had finally found the purpose of my life, a secret had been revealed. I knew the reason why I had come into this world. There was so much to be done. My mind was swirling. I told Sheraz to leave me alone, and that I had to do some detail thinking. I closed myself in Baba's study, with little Selma playing in the corner of the room while I began to put down this dream on paper, and ink it with reality.

First, I had to find donors for this huge project. Then I would have to register this dream and give it a name.

I was so busy, way out there in my thoughts, that I didn't realize it was way past lunch time.

Selma came running to me, and began to shake my arm and said, "I'm hungry."

I held her close to me and she in turn gazed up at me and said, "You know what I like best about being here? When you hug me, I feel I am in the arms of my mother."

That was it; I had a name now, "IN THE ARMS

OF A MOTHER."

Next day, Sheraz and I went to the registrar's office, and got all the paperwork done. The name of the place was "IN THE ARMS OF A MOTHER," a shelter home for girls, founded by Selma Abid – the name of my dearest friend – and funded by generous mothers all over the world.

Everything seemed perfect. Calls began to come in from all my friends, and they all donated generously. We started to extend the house, to add boarding rooms and bathrooms. We didn't want to go fancy, for we wanted to save the money for the actual needs of these girls. Sheraz came up with a very good idea, and suggested that we should have a small classroom where these girls could study, and for those who wanted to go to school we would pay their fees and send them to good schools. I knew that in today's world, educating women was the key to their betterment. I had two more years before Nadia came back from Egypt, and then I would have to return to London.

The day the name board was put up was a very emotional day for me. I touched Selma's name written on the marble slab and for the first time, I felt that I had made Selma proud of me, that she had finally taught me the lesson of courage, and living for others.

The construction was in full swing. Sheraz was a big help. I couldn't have done this without him. Dealing with all these local workers would have been impossible for me. In midst of all the noise of the construction, I started to take long walks, which helped me think with a clear mind. On one such walk, I decided that it was now time to write the book about my journey through life. There was so much that was unspoken in my life, I wanted to at least write it down. I didn't know if I would ever complete this book, or when, or what the end would be, but I started to write. I was actually enjoying myself in Lucknow, and the strain or fear of running into Yusuf didn't scare me anymore. I knew I wouldn't fall apart.

My old school, where Selma and I use to study, was under repair, so little Selma and I would sneak in through the broken gate, and sit under that banyan tree. This is where I started to write my book. I felt this place was a big part of my life story. After a long day of satisfying writing, I would take little Selma to her now-favorite place, Ghasitaram Sweet Mart. The name had changed and the owner too, but the flavor was still the same. The jalebees were still hot and juicy, with cold cream on them, and the samosas were as spicy as ever. I never understood why I became so attached to this little child; was it because of her name? Sometimes I felt maybe she was a reincarnation of Selma, or perhaps Selma had sent her to me, to calm my soul, or to make me feel that she had never left me. It felt nice to be able to walk through the past. After all, the past doesn't come back, but sometimes one can go back and visit it.

Every evening Nadia would call me from Egypt, and update me on her studies and discoveries. One day she sounded very excited, and told me she had met a Pakistani boy in the café which she visited often. His name was Ahmed. She said that they got into an argument, and for the first time someone had changed her point of view. Nadia was quite headstrong, and impulsive. That she actually listened to someone's advice was surprising but very comforting for me. I thought finally she was maturing.

Ahmed had come to Egypt on a company assignment, and would be there for a year or so. He had done his masters in finance. Ahmed seemed like a good boy. He had been orphaned at the age of eleven, when his parents died in a plane crash. Since then, Ahmed lived with his elder brother, who had now settled in London. It was so strange that Ahmed had studied in London and was working there for so many years, but we never met. His brother's home was about two hours' drive from our home. Destiny made them meet on foreign soil, and they fell in love.

I was so enthralled when they both confessed to me that they wanted to get married. The wedding was to be held two weeks after Nadia returned from Egypt. I was happy and nervous at the same time – how would I do all this? My daughter was getting married; I kept repeating this line again and again, still it wouldn't sink in. She was my little baby till now, and I had not come to terms with the fact that one day she too would leave.

Nadia had expressed this desire that I do all her shopping from India. She wanted a wedding filled with Indian culture, and that meant an elaborate one. In our culture the wedding goes on for a week or so, with various ceremonies that are not religious, but fun. Life felt so perfect, I was doing everything I always wanted to do.

By now, we had six girls residing in the shelter. Some were from very poor homes who had been abandoned, and the police or the social worker would come and leave them here. There was one girl whose name was Fatima. Fatima was an orphan, and had stayed in an orphanage from age six. She had come to us to ask us if she could stay in our shelter home. We asked her why she wanted to come here, since she was already being taken care of at the orphanage. Fatima seemed very reluctant to go back, she was terrified. I didn't want to refuse her shelter, so we let her stay. She didn't talk much for a few weeks, but finally she confessed to me that she was being molested by the orphanage manager, Jagan Singh.

But there was something worse than that which she needed to spill out.

Fatima later on told me that she had killed the manager with a kitchen knife and had run away. She was thirteen now, and if she hadn't killed him, he would have gotten her pregnant. She had no other choice because he wouldn't let her go out alone, so that she couldn't complain to anyone. She had left this onus on my shoulders, and I was the one to decide if she should be surrendered to the police, for protecting herself, or not. I knew her story was very heart-wrenching and true, but the matter of fact was that she had killed someone.

I consulted one of Baba's old lawyer friends. He

told me what the legality was, but I kept thinking about the humane aspect of this situation. I knew if she went to the police they would put her in jail forever, or there would be a humiliating long trial to prove that her act was in self defense. In any case her life would not get better. The orphanage was not very far from our shelter, they would find her easily. Fatima was turning hysterical with fear and guilt. She looked like a bird trapped in a cage. Suddenly she became quiet and I could hear only sniffles. When I went into the room to see what had finally calmed her, I saw her clinging to Sheraz, and Sheraz kept consoling her, "I'll take care of you, no one will hurt you anymore." I was speechless. Sheraz looked up at me and said that today he too had found the reason why God had sent him down to this world.

I had a detailed talk with Sheraz and told him, "This could not be done, she has committed a murder, an unforgivable crime."

Sheraz turned around and told me, "People commit so many sins and crime and go scot free. If she has done wrong to protect herself and many more like her by killing a rascal, then let's leave it to God. If God wants her to be punished she will be, otherwise she too can get lost amongst the herds of million. Who cares anyway? There are millions who never receive justice, so let her be the one innocent who didn't get punished." I was sold on that last note and we decided to let life take its own course.

The construction of the shelter was nearly over, and Fatima had become an integral part of our home. She had been with us for six months and no one had inquired. Sheraz did read news clippings about the murder of an orphanage manager. The media claimed that it was the work of some money lenders, whose debt he had not returned.

There was never any news of a missing girl – after all, who cares about an orphan girl? The real story was that the NGOs who were running this orphanage had received many complaints from the other employees about the manager's sexual misconduct. It was better to close this chapter respectfully, and blame it on something benign.

The next few weeks were spent in never-ending wedding shopping for Nadia, but it was so much fun. I would be out for the whole day with Selma and Fatima as my little helpers. We enjoyed shopping and treats, and often on the way, dreams and fears were expressed over a glass of ice cold lassi, a refreshing Indian yogurt shake. Selma still had nightmares about collecting the pieces of her parent's bodies, and Fatima lived in constant fear of being found. Gradually, due to the happy environment around them, the past became fainter and they began to look ahead.

Fatima had a sharp mind. She had done some schooling at the orphanage, and she wanted to finish high school. I was a little hesitant to send her to a regular school; they might need information about her parents and past. Sheraz offered to teach her, and then she could appear privately for the test. Selma was very playful, and just wanted to have fun, but I put her in a school and told her how important it was for her to be educated. Sheraz and Fatima were an inseparable team. I didn't have to worry about the daily affairs of the shelter; they had a grasp on everything that needed to be done, and got all the jobs done on time.

It had been a year now since we had started this shelter. We had about nineteen girls residing in the home, and it was getting really crammed. After awareness of the shelter had spread around the city, a lot of girls came in themselves. Most of them were in bad shape, and really needed shelter and counseling.

There were a few girls from well to do families, but they had suffered incest and other abuses. They just needed to be away from that environment until they were able to stand on their own feet, and be independent. Our doors were open for all, and it was difficult to refuse any girl, but we saw to it that no one was trying to take advantage of our free boarding and lodging. I needed more funding to build an annexed building, and we had the land. We started to look for local sponsors. People tried to help in whatever way they could. We would receive concessions on food and clothing. Every little bit helped. But I never wanted my girls to work, since to help the residents of the shelter was the responsibility of the community. These were our sisters and daughters in need.

Nadia would be returning soon, and I would have to return to London.

In fact it was good timing, since going to London I could get Nadia married and be free of responsibilities, and also collect the much-needed funding for our new building. A week later we received the immigration papers for Sheraz's visa, and now he could come with me to London. I was very happy that everything was falling into the right place. I informed Sheraz about his visa, and told him to start packing his stuff because we would be leaving soon. Fatima and a new lady manager we had hired could take care of the shelter, and I could oversee all the work remotely.

The manager we had hired for the shelter was called Abida. She was a pro bono lawyer, and wanted to do something that really mattered. There had to be an adult woman around, to watch and guide these girls when I wasn't around. Things had quite stabilized now at the shelter; everything was running smoothly, and we were getting recognized, and finally making a difference. Every night before bed time, I would go into the girl's dorm, and sit and chat with them. The topics were varied, often about the day's happenings, and sometimes very intense details about past bleeding wounds were discussed.

I would often feel at a loss over giving the most appropriate advice. Before I left I wanted to have a counselor on board, someone these girls could share their horrible experiences with and get correct and professional advice on how to move ahead.

Three days later at a grocery store, I met Sheela, who lived about six miles away from the shelter. Sheela was a counselor by profession, and a sitar teacher by hobby. All my life I had wanted to learn the sitar; she was God-sent.

Every evening, for the three weeks till I left for

London, Sheela taught me the sitar. During our lessons, I would discuss our shelter with Sheela about, how we could benefit from her professional help. It turned out that Sheela herself was an orphan, and was very eager to help. Seeing me learn the sitar, a lot of the other girls showed interest. So it was decided that Sheela had two jobs here, and everyone was happy, especially Sheela.

I told Nadia about my sitar, and she was so happy for me. I told her that as soon as I came back after her wedding, I would learn the sitar to my heart's content and finish writing my book.

For once, Nadia was very proud of me, and said, "Mom, its time you start living your life."

I added, "Yah, before it's too late." I was happy that God was being so kind to me; I felt blessed.

The irony was that I had been in Lucknow for nearly two years now and the shelter was so close to Yusuf's home, but I never met him, or bumped into him, and they say the world is a small place. The most amazing thing was that this didn't bother me at all. Sheraz had learnt that Yusuf had moved into an apartment in the main city. We would go to the city every so often, but my eyes had stopped searching for Yusuf, and I never did see him.

Everyone was upset that Sheraz and I were leaving for London. They feared that we wouldn't come back. It was tough to convince them that they would not be abandoned again.

Just before the day we were to leave, Sheraz knocked at my door. It was very late, and I was worried. Sheraz came in looking much frazzled. He sat down beside my bed, and began apologizing to me and weeping. He told me to my great surprise that he would not be going to London with me. Last evening he had taken Fatima to the mosque and there they were married. He and Fatima wanted to stay here and take care of the shelter.

I smiled at him lovingly and said, "Who's going to help me there with Nadia's wedding in London?" We both laughed and hugged each other. Fatima, who was now fifteen years old, had been standing all this time outside my door; she came in shyly and hugged me. I gave both of them my blessing, and told Sheraz that I was proud of him. They told me that they would be living in Mamu's house, but they would continue to take care of the shelter.

The whole team came to see me off at the airport. Sheraz had rented two minivans for all the girls, who kept weeping all the way to the airport. I convinced them that I would be back soon after two months.

During my plane ride back I felt so lonely. I had been surrounded with so many people for the last two years. Everyone in the plane was sleeping, and the lights had been turned off, but I couldn't sleep. My heart was very restless. There was this dire need to finish my book. Without analyzing the feeling too much, I dug into my hand bag, and took out my notebook. During the last two years, I had completed quite a bit of my life's journey. I had nearly reached my present time. I began to write, and I wrote voraciously. There was some kind of indescribable fear that was strongly urging me to finish my story soon. I wrote and wrote throughout the entire eighteen-hour flight. When we landed in London, I was exhausted, but felt very content. It had been a rough ride, but right now I was happy, because I was finally getting my chance to live. It was nice coming back home. London felt like home now, and India had become my second home. I had a week to settle in before Nadia would be back from Egypt, and I was waiting eagerly for her.

22

PRESENT TIME

It was around 8 am and last night had left me exhausted. To take a walk through one's past has never been easy. I felt so jaded and it felt like I had actually lived a lifetime in those few hours. I looked at myself in the mirror, and realized how much I had changed. It all started to come back to me. I had come back from India after three years, where I had started the shelter. Nadia was back from Egypt, and was to be married in two weeks, and worst of all, I had seen Yusuf at the London airport. It was the weirdest thing. I had been in India for three years, and never met Yusuf there. Here, as soon as I came back I see him right in front of my face at the airport. Destiny was playing a cruel game with me.

My image in the mirror kept staring back at me, and taunting me. I was too confused, I didn't know what to do. I wasn't very sure if I wanted to check

Unspoken

on Yusuf at the hospital. After all, he didn't even recognize me at the airport. But finally seeing Yusuf after so many years was shattering the wall I had built around me.

Nadia was still asleep, so I started breakfast. Sheraz called from India and said that due to some new laws passed recently, Sheela wanted me to sign some legal property papers. I asked Sheraz to send them to me by speed post, and I would return them.

Ahmed and his family would be arriving tonight and I had to start preparations for dinner, too. They would be staying in a hotel close by till the wedding, since it would be awkward for the groom's people to stay at the bride's home. I composed myself so that I could come back to what was on hand right now. I started making a grocery list for the Indian market. I would get some food catered for the wedding and some I would cook. Nadia woke up starving around 10 am, and she had the good, healthy breakfast that I had prepared. I told her I was going for groceries, and would be back in two to three hours. Nadia's wedding had made me very happy, everything else became so bearable. She would be able to marry the man she loved.

As I drove to the market, I saw a sign for Hilling-don hospital. Why did I have to look at it? Destiny was leading me, and on an impulse I turned my car towards that direction, as if I was hypnotized and had no control. I was still very angry and furious. I thought Yusuf did need to know how he had destroyed my life, and how he had soured my relationship with my dear Baba. I was doing something that my heart was making me do, because my mind had totally shut down. I wanted to slap Yusuf, or hurt him the way he had hurt me. I couldn't forgive him for destroying me; he did not deserve that mercy. My heart wanted to ask him, why did he have to enslave me, why did he leave me to bleed forever? When had I ever wronged Yusuf? I had only loved him from the depth of my heart; why then did he have to punish me this way? I could no longer cloak my desire to meet him one last time.

    I parked in the hospital visitor's lot, and started to tread nervously towards the reception desk. It was so difficult for me to even say his name after so many years, for his name had been confined within the boundaries of my heart. I was scared his name would make me cry, as it had for the last twenty-five years. I did not want to cry anymore. I had to just bleed my heart in front of him, and drain out his existence from my veins.

The hospital receptionist pointed me to the next wing, room 42. I realized I was sweating profusely, even though it was freezing outside. My long black hair was sticking to my waist, and I felt as if I was walking through a death chamber, and very soon my sentence would be declared.

Outside the room, about five men from India were standing and they all seemed very nervous. One of the men saw me standing near the room. He came up to me and asked if I was here to see Yusuf. I was startled because I was just trying to peer into the room. All I needed was a few seconds with Yusuf. I did not need to talk to anyone else. I felt as if I had made a mistake by being there. I feared that someone would recognize me. They would ask me questions, many questions.

That man then asked if I was related to Yusuf. I really didn't know how to answer that question. I was too old to be a fan of his and so I nervously said, "My father knew him. We used to be neighbors in Lucknow. I had seen him fall sick at the airport, that's how I came here." I don't know why, but that man looked at me very weirdly, as if he didn't believe me. He asked me to wait, then went back to his friends and started to whisper to them. One of the gentlemen, who seemed to be the oldest amongst them, came to me. He told me he was one of the organizers of the poetry recital for which Yusuf had been invited here. He very plainly informed me that Yusuf had just passed away from a massive cardiac arrest. He kept talking to me and lamenting how expensive things were there, the hospital bill and then the burial. But I wasn't listening to him. I kept staring at his face intensely, trying to recreate what he had just told me.

For a moment my heart stopped pounding, so that my mind could hear what this man was saying.

He told me that Yusuf had no one back in India who would claim his body, and that it was too expensive to transport the body back to India. He went on to explain that some of them had pooled in and paid the hospital bill, since they wouldn't release the body till the dues were cleared. Still, there was the need to pay for the transport of the body to a local Muslim cemetery, and then there would also be the burial charges.

He wasn't asking me for money, but merely expressing his difficulty. He then left me alone and went back to his group of friends.

It took me few very long seconds till it finally sank in, that the man I had loved, was no more in this world. Yusuf had died, and I couldn't say anything. I didn't know how to react. The pain that my heart had borne for endless years had finally numbed my heart. I had come all this way to tell him that I had loved him, and that in return he had only destroyed my life. But Yusuf as always was not around to hear my pleas; he had finally left me. I had not been able to confess my love to him; God had once again saved me. Yusuf did not deserve to know that there had been someone who had honestly loved him. I trembled with this shame and realization.

I could overhear those men, trying to arrange for some charitable ambulance service. I felt this was one last thing I needed to do for Yusuf. I took out my checkbook from my purse. I had 500 pounds that Abbas had given to me on our wedding day, and I had never used that money. I wrote a check for the same amount, and gave it to the man. He looked at the check and then looked at me. He was a very honest man. He thanked me profusely, and politely said it was much more money than was needed to cover the expenses. I smiled and said, "Take good care of his burial, and whatever money is left, you could donate it." I felt as if I had paid him to bury my crime, and my imprisonment was finally over.

I started to walk away, feeling very unburdened and free. The man kept calling out to me, asking me if I wanted to see Yusuf's dead body and pay my last respects. I didn't need to see him anymore. All my life I was chained to his heart, never to his body. Now his heart had stopped beating, and my heart was finally set free. As I walked away I felt a sharp twitch in my heart, as if a vein had snapped, and I let my heart bleed for the last time. Yusuf was no more in this world and no more in my heart.

Walking down the hospital stairs, I felt a weird warmth in my body. I could hear my heart beat as if someone had blown life into it. I was so proud of myself, I didn't shed a tear, I didn't fall apart. Even today, after twenty-five years, I never let anyone know about the love I had for Yusuf. I sat in my car, and tried to comprehend all that had just happened. Yusuf had left this world, but then, he could have died anywhere. Why did he have to die in London, and also be seen by me? This was his first trip to London, and he had to die in my neighborhood, millions of miles away from his home. Perhaps my call of love for him was finally answered. Yusuf *did* come to me, and he was here to stay, this brought an impish smile to my face.

I had wasted precious years of my life waiting for him. This storm called Yusuf had resurfaced once again on my shore, but it could no longer destroy me. Every wave of emotion for him had subsided. There was nothing but a deep, calm stillness; the grey clouds were clearing and I could see the sunlight again. My imprisonment was over, and I felt I could breathe and live my life. I had caged Yusuf in my heart for twenty-five years, and in doing so had destroyed my very being. Death finally setting him free had also unshackled my heart forever.

They began to load the body in the ambulance. My car was parked a few rows away from the exit. As the ambulance was leaving the hospital, that same elderly man saw me. He stopped the ambulance, got down, and came over and introduced himself as Shakil. He handed me a business card and assured me that he appreciated what I had done – it was a great act of humanity. He asked me if I wanted to follow them to the cemetery so that I could witness Yusuf's final departure from this world.

Now that this man had declared me to be a good human being, going to the cemetery wouldn't do me any harm. Weirdly, I actually wanted to be sure of Yusuf's departure from this world.

On reaching the cemetery I stood away from the grave site, as women in our culture are not allowed near the grave. There were just five strangers attending Yusuf's funeral, and now I too was a stranger to him.

This man who was now lying so still and lifeless in his grave had taught my heart to beat, and to bleed willingly for him. I was like a slave to him. Yet today he lay there, helpless and unloved.

After everyone left, Shakil came over to me, and thanked me once again for doing such a great work of charity. As Shakil and the rest of his friends were leaving, I began to walk slowly towards Yusuf's grave.

The gravedigger was closing up the grave. It was so barren: no flowers, no loved ones standing and saying prayers to save his soul.

The gravedigger looked at me consolingly and said, "You can take your time, I am done here."

I had no more prayer for Yusuf. I had drained my heart over a span of a lifetime. I went and plucked a branch from a birch tree which was shading a nearby grave, and I placed this branch on Yusuf's grave.

I remembered that Mom had told me once that

everything in this universe – birds, animals, flowers and trees – send praise to the Almighty every second. Hence when loved ones visit grave sites, they leave flowers there, so that while they are gone, the flowers will keep praying for the departed soul.

Since Yusuf had no one to pray for him, and I knew he would definitely need it in his afterworld, I left that branch on his grave, hoping that at least its frail leaves would pray for him. Here lay the man for whom I had waited a lifetime, now lifeless at my feet.

I finally said that which I wanted to say to him for so many years: "Goodbye Yusuf." Once I whispered these words, I felt as if there was a load lifted off my heart; it was beating freely, as if I was twenty-one again.

There was a kind of sprint in my feet as I walked towards my car, I kept crying and laughing at the same time. I had not betrayed love, I had loved and my love was true. It didn't matter that the person I loved was wrong; what mattered was that he had made me aware of my intense ability to love.

I was free now; I could live now with a heart beating in my chest, and not a hollow. I didn't know how to express this, but I knew I was alive, and I wanted to live. I didn't have to hide Yusuf from anyone. He was dead, and that made it weirdly safe to tell anyone that I was in love with him once. After all, how could a dead person come and ruin your reputation? I could share the secret of my heart, I could tell Nadia and I was sure she would understand me.

Nadia's name brought me back from my past. I had come out to do shopping for Nadia's guest tonight. As I hurried towards my car, I saw Mr. Shakil still standing there behind a tree. I looked at him suspiciously. He just nodded his head in greeting, and said he was waiting to pay the gravedigger. I sat in my car, and began to drive. Once again I met my eyes in my rear view mirror. My eyes were brimming with tears, but my lips were smiling, and in a few seconds, my eyes were smiling too.

I thought I never looked so beautiful or so happy.

I began to realize that it was because of Abbas' love that I was able to survive this torment, which in my illusion was love. I realized I had been so gullible and naive. I guess that's what Yusuf had taken advantage of.

I hated myself for wasting my love on him. Experiences, not age, makes one wise. It is so pathetic that some people spend their whole life running after a shadow. Nothing is more precious than life, because there is no replacement, there is only one life. There was so much I wanted to do with my life and prayed, May God give me enough time.

23

The Mid Town Asian market was located on 3rd and 7th street. I parked my car in their vast parking lot, and began to climb those treacherous stone steps. These were the steps that would take one from the parking lot to the three levels of this open market. On the first level were all the restaurants, the second level was fresh produce and the flower market, and the third level had the clothing section. Every time I had to climb these steps, my knees would rebel. There were six solid stone steps, with an iron railing on both sides.

Today I was so happy, I felt I could run and skip over these steps. First I visited Tandoor Restaurant. I had to check on the food that they were to cater at the wedding. When you enter an Indian restaurant you get engulfed in a sea of aromas. Satish the manager convinced me that everything was in place, and nothing would go wrong. I paid him some advance money on the order, just to keep them motivated.

Next to Tandoor was Bombay Chaat House, a famous fast food or street food restaurant. They sold my favorite snacks from my childhood: samosas, jalebees, and chaat.

I couldn't resist the temptation, and I bought some samosas and jalebees. I rationalized my indulgence, telling myself that Ahmed and his family would also love these snacks. So I took some extras for the evening party. In the next level I bought some veggies that I needed for tonight's dinner. Everything seemed so fresh and vibrant, as if I was looking at it for the very first time.

It suddenly dawned on me that due to my diversion to the hospital, I had been out of the house far longer than I had estimated. I knew I wouldn't have enough time to cook dinner. It was already 4 pm, and the sun was beginning to set.

I called Satish from the vegetable vender's store, and asked him to pack some meat dishes, which I would pick up on my way down to my car. I had always been so nervous organizing parties, but today everything felt like a breeze. As I was passing the flower market, I thought I should also remind them about the flower decorations I had ordered for the wedding.

Flowers have always been my greatest passion. No matter how down I was feeling, flowers always would cheer me up. I remember when I was single, I used to talk to all the flowers in our garden. Selma and everyone else thought I was crazy, but it gave me a lot of peace. As I entered the market, I could see an array of different flowers, some very common and some were very unique. My eyes settled on one such flower, the champa. I was so happy that they had started to sell it everywhere in London. The florist told me that someone had specially ordered them for a prayer ceremony. I pleaded with him to let me have one.

He humored me and gave me a very healthy and full champa. I at once placed it delicately in my hair. Its fragrance lulled every sense of mine. Sweet memories of my mom and dad flashed in my eyes. It was very strange, but for the first time I felt as beautiful as my mother. Just as I was gloating in my beauty, Nadia called at the florist and asked if I was still around. I told her everything had been well arranged, and even though I was running late, everything would be perfect.

Nadia asked, "Mom are you okay? You have never sounded so positive and relaxed."

I told her, "I'm just happy to be alive." She knew I was delaying my trip at the flower market. There was so much I wanted to tell her, but not on the phone, and not now, because it was her special time.

I really didn't have any business in the clothes section, except to pick up Nadia's blouse that I had left there for stitching. A beautiful chiffon sari grabbed my attention as I passed by one boutique. It was in the front display window, and I felt as if it had been designed for me. The base was a deep burgundy, and a light brown branch ran across it, which was filled with brown sequins. In between the brown branches, a few light green leaves were sown. These too had been embroidered with sequins and silk thread.

It reminded me of autumn, my favorite season. I impulsively went in and asked the price; it was quite expensive, and I had already done tons of shopping in India. But it was just too perfect, and I was too happy to let anything spoil my mood today. I bought it. I think this was the first time I had ever indulged in me. It felt so good to do something for me.

The climb down from the top level was going to be awkward. I had so much stuff in my hands: my sari, snacks, Nadia's clothes, and some beautiful fresh tube lilies I had bought to celebrate the occasion. I went to the restaurant to pick up the dishes for tonight. Satish said that they were not ready, and he would have them delivered to my home in one hour.

Everything was in place; the wedding would definitely be perfect. I was so pleased with myself, and so happy for Nadia. She was getting to marry the man she loved, and who loved her too. I think God was being a little too kind to me, but I was enjoying it. The samosas smelt so good, I felt like opening up the package and eating one. Just then, in a fraction of a second, my dress got caught in my sandals, and I missed just one step.

In an instant I was rolling down the steps, out of control, my head hitting hard on each step and then slashing on to the iron railing. I tried frantically to hold on to something, everything flung out from my hands and was tumbling down with me. I stopped only at the end of the stairway. I lay flat on my back, on the now cold and hard parking lot ground.

I knew I was badly hurt, because I couldn't feel anything. My back was very cold and wet, it was the blood from my head that was draining the life out of me. I lay there still and numbed, and all I could see was the deep blue sky. I could faintly hear people approaching and gathering around me. They were trying to ask me something, but I couldn't hear them. Suddenly the deep blue sky became very colorful. I felt as if I was looking through a kaleidoscope. It was so beautiful; the blue color of the sky had mixed with the deep red of my blood that was now flowing across my face and eyes, creating these magical colors. It reminded me of the colorful street light at the Aminabad market in Lucknow.

I felt as if I was lying in my father's lap, watching these lights, and gradually slipping into a deep sleep. The fragrance of the champa, still clinging to my hair, drenched in my blood, made me feel as if Mom was very close to me. I was at peace, all my senses were fading away, everything was becoming dim and bleak, and suddenly, darkness was complete.

As I shut my eyes for the last time, I heard my feeble breath whisper, "BABA."

Part II
NADIA

24

It was around 8 pm that evening when two police officers arrived at our home; they informed me that my mother, Mrs. Sharmeen Bakhtiar, had passed away. My fiancé Ahmed and his family had been waiting impatiently for my mother to return from the Asian market. The two officers kept describing the ghastly death that Mom had gone through. Ahmed was trying desperately to concentrate on what the police had to say, but all his attention was drawn towards me. I was standing strengthless, holding on to some piece of furniture for support. I could only dare to read this fearful story through the pain in Ahmed's eyes. I knew it wasn't a nightmare that I would wake up from; this was actually happening, and I would have to live through it.

I broke my fear-induced silence by asking aloud, "Where is my mother now?" and then I broke down hysterically. The next three hours, I was insane with trauma, nobody could control me. Finally Ahmed called in a doctor, and I was sedated. Late that night, about 4 am, Ahmed came and woke me up. He said that the police had called, and that they wanted us to come to the morgue, to identify the body. I was grateful that I had been sedated, because in no other condition could I ever have been able do this.

We drove up to the morgue, and as soon as I got out of the car, an eerie feeling of death lingered all around. Even the air seemed so heavy and damp, as if one couldn't breathe in it.

Ahmed held my hand, and was literally dragging me to see the final eventuality of my nightmare. There, surrounded by pristine white tiles, the air heady with the smell of Dettol, and sanitizers, as if someone had just been born, I saw a white shroud covering a slim figure, lying in the center of an empty room.

The doctor said that I had to be aware that the face had been brutally damaged by the stone steps, and that bones had been crushed. On hearing that, I got extremely nauseous. I gathered my courage and I told Ahmed that I couldn't see her this way. I want to remember her with her beautiful, smiling face.

Ahmed concurred, and went ahead to identify the body of my mother. He didn't have to tell me anything; I knew it was her, I could sense her all around me, and it was too overwhelming to be expressed in words. All the paperwork was done by Ahmed, so that the body could be given its final resting place. I sat outside in the waiting area. There was no one there, except dead silence. My eyes couldn't stop crying, and searching this emptiness for a glimpse of my mother.

On our drive back home, Ahmed told me that he would call the Muslim cemetery in the city and ask them to make arrangements for the funeral. He kept talking about what arrangements had to be made, and that I needed to participate, at least for the blessing of my mother's soul.

I looked at him lovingly and said, "I will, but don't call the Muslim cemetery because Mom and Dad both did not like that place. I think Mom should be buried at the countryside cemetery where Dad was buried." Ahmed and everyone else agreed that Mom would have wanted that. After reaching home, the frenzy of making phone calls for the funeral, started. When Ahmed called the countryside cemetery, to inform them, that we would be bringing mom there, he asked if a plot next to my father's grave was still empty. To his utter surprise, the manager said, "It had been booked by Sharmeen Bakhtiar, a few years after her husband passed away." She had loved this cemetery a lot, and on one of her visits to Dad's grave, she must have decided that she too would want to be buried there, right next to the man who loved her to the last moment of his life.

I met many new faces on the day of my mom's funeral. I was amazed that people were so fond of her, and that, she had made so many friends. People not only loved her, but respected her. Everyone was so compassionate that they all were treating me as if I was their own daughter; that all felt so honest.

I had not known this social side of Mom, because I was too busy with my own life, but it made me feel proud to be her daughter. A lot of people called from India to give condolence. Everyone from Mom's shelter in India felt shattered. They all spoke to me as if they knew me so well. I told Sheraz that he would have to manage the shelter for a while, till I settled things here. I assured him that we would sit down together and discuss how to keep Mom's mission alive. I really didn't know what I was saying, or how I would be able to do the things that Mom had done, but it gave real stillness to my heart, when I said it. Mom was finally buried, and lay next to the man she had loved and who loved her immensely.

Uncle Shabir, who was now eighty-six, advised me with tearful eyes that Ahmed and I should not delay our marriage. He said this was Mom's greatest wish, to see me settled and happy. Uncle Shabir gave me away to Ahmed, at a quiet, small, and simple ceremony in our mosque. Even though Mom had gone, life wouldn't stop, and we had to keep moving with it because we were still alive. I had not accepted Mom's death, and I don't think any child can.

Ahmed had his own apartment a few blocks away from Mom's house, and we settled in there. I knew I would have to sell Mom's house, as it would be very difficult to maintain two homes. We decided that whatever money we would get from the house we would donate it to Mom's shelter.

Life was moving at a very slow pace. We had been married for about three months now, but everything, every desire seemed incomplete, all because I could no longer share my life with Mom.

One day when I was too overwhelmed with memories, I went to visit Mom's home. It looked as if it had been abandoned. I started to clean up the cobwebs and the dust. In the corner where the letter box hung, some mail had spilled out from the now overflowing, unchecked pile. I gathered a handful, and began to sort through it. There were some legal papers about Mom's life insurance and the trust fund that she and Dad had left for me. I just pushed them aside unopened. I don't know why I kept hoping that there might be a letter from Mom. Parents carve a very deep niche in the hearts of their children, and even if life parts them from us, they stay alive and immortal in our souls. We are a part of them, the still living part.

Amongst the various insignificant letters, there was one which seemed that it didn't belong here. It was sent from a cultural organization, the "South Asia cultural group," and it was addressed to Mom. I opened the letter very hesitantly, as I knew she hadn't been connected to any cultural group. There was a receipt for a check received in the amount of 500 pounds, and dated exactly the day mom had died. A letter was attached with the receipt, that read,

"Thank you Madame for your kind donation, which as per your wishes, was used for the final burial expenses of Mr. Yusuf Ali. We have included you as one of our prominent donors, and will be sending you complementary passes for our future shows. As per your instructions, the leftover amount of 200 pounds was donated to an orphanage in India. Thank you, Shakil Abbasi."

This was very weird to me – why would Mom donate such a generous amount to a music group, and most of all, who was Yusuf Ali?

I called uncle Shabir; he said he didn't know any Yusuf Ali whom Mom knew. I don't know why, but this name bothered me a lot. I went to the given address on the letter. It was on Kent Street, near the Asian market. The office was a very small, junky, make-shift kind of place. I hoped that Mom had not been swindled. Inside, an unreasonably fat man sat at the reception desk. I asked for Mr. Shakil. I was shown into a very dimly lit room, with drab curtains that smelt of fungus and dampness. I could vaguely see an elderly man sitting on a chair desk, talking on the phone very loudly in Urdu. After he hung up, he apologized to me for talking so loudly, saying he was on the phone with someone in India.

He then very politely and expectantly asked me if I was there to buy tickets for the next show, or to make a donation. I didn't want to fall into any more traps, so I came directly to the point, and showed him the receipt that he had sent to Mom. He looked at the receipt, then read it out aloud, and looked at me very confused. He asked me who I was, and what did I want to know. I did not realize that this complete stranger was going to open the curtain to my mom's past. I told him that I was Sharmeen Bakhtiar's daughter, the one who had given him this check. Mr. Shakil stood up respectfully, and greeted me again. He said that he had seen very few selfless and humane people like my mother. Shakil went on to praise my mother till I interrupted him and gave him the news of her death. Shakil was shocked and just fell back in his chair. He was in utter disbelief. He kept saying that he had seen her a few months ago and that she looked healthy. Then I told him about Mom's freaky accident – the same day that she had given him this check, that same evening she died. I was trying to retrace her steps, to find out how she had spent her last day. Also I desperately wanted to know who Yusuf Ali was.

Mr. Shakil told me all the details: who Yusuf was, and how he died, and how Mom had given them the much-needed money to bury him. He also told me where Yusuf was buried, and that Mom had stayed there till the very end to place the branch on his grave. Even Shakil did not know how Yusuf was related to Mom. He knew he was from Lucknow, and he said that Mom had told him that they had been neighbors there.

I thought to myself, as I drove back home, this man had to be very dear to Mom, otherwise why would she attend his funeral, especially on the day when there was something so important about my marriage going on at home. That's why Mom had been so late in going to the Asian market.

I was starting to put the pieces together of Mom's final moments. The biggest piece of the puzzle was Yusuf Ali. When I reached home, Ahmed and I discussed the matter. Ahmed, teasingly, said, "Maybe Yusuf might have been mom's secret lover; after all she was so pretty." I glared at him so hard that he miraculously came up with a brilliant idea.

He said, "Why don't you call Sheraz in India? I'm sure he lives there, and he might have known Yusuf." Sheraz gave me a lot of details about Yusuf being my grandfather's friend and poet, and that Mom knew him because of her dad. I thought it was a very grand gesture on mom's part, to favor an old neighbor and a friend of her dad like this. With that, I left the matter unresolved.

A year later, we got the first offer for Mom's home, and I was pregnant with our first child. It was predicted to be a girl. We had decided to name her Sana. During my fourth month, there was a final deal for the house, which we accepted. Then came the big task of emptying out the house. I had told Ahmed that we would take Mom's favorite furniture into our apartment. I had always loved her dresser, from the time I was a little girl. Mom had ordered it from Lucknow. Uncle Shabir told me that it had belonged to my grandmother, Yasmeen Kazi. It was made of solid teakwood, with a dark mahogany polish. The whole dresser had intricate carvings, done by hand. It was really an antique, a piece that had witnessed a lot of history. The mirror had gone a little foggy at certain places, especially where the sun danced on it most mornings. That was the first piece of furniture that I sent to my apartment. Everything had a memory attached to it, but there were too many pieces. Mom had loved to collect artistic furniture. She also had a delicate black cherry tea table, with two chairs. I remember Dad telling me how Mom had brought this from a quaint shop in the Chinese market.

I touched the glass top gently, and I could hear the echoes of my own childish voice, arguing with Mom over my homework. Mom and I would sit on this table every evening after school. She would ask me to show her my work, as she sipped her hot cup of chai. This table too had very fond memories spilled all over it. I hoped that one day I would sit with my daughter, share a cup of chai, and make some memories.

I went into Mom's bedroom, where everything was as she had left it. This room was still filled with her fragrance and presence. I sat on her bed, it was cold. I remember most nights before going to sleep I would jump into Mom's bed, and cuddle up in her blanket. Somehow her bed felt as warm and compassionate as her. I had left this house in such a rush, to avoid facing reality, that the bed sheets on Mom's bed hadn't even been changed. In the chaos of the movers, who were moving the stuff out from the house, I found peace and calm on Mom's pillow. It was still fragrant with her presence.

Under her pillow I found a black diary. I had never seen it before, but I remembered that Mom had once mentioned to me that she had started to write. After reading a few pages, I realized that it was Mom's life story. I felt a rush of emotion, as if I had found something that I needed. I was so enthralled, I felt as if Mom had come back to me. I held it in my hands – my mother's precious life, and all its secrets. I began to cry, but the emptiness of the room reminded me that my mother was not there.

I had not realized till then, that I knew so little about my mother. I felt she had gone too soon, just like Dad, and loneliness had entered into my world.

We had to move the stuff out and give the house keys to the new owners by evening. I reluctantly stopped reading Mom's book, as Ahmed was constantly complaining, that he was starving.

As I walked out of that house for the last time, holding onto Mom's book, I felt, I was carrying the very soul of the house with me. There was nothing left in this house now, only bricks and wood, and I could let go of it. Next week the deal was signed and the money was paid. I did not want to even know how much we had made on this house. I asked Ahmed to transfer the money to Mom's account in India, for the shelter.

I called Sheraz, and told him about the funds, and explained that they didn't need to worry about expenses. While we talked, Sheraz mentioned to me the book that Mom had started to write in Lucknow. He asked me how much of it was complete, and said that I should complete it now for Mom, and have it published. I had completely forgotten about the book; there was so much happening, so quickly, that I was off balance. I know I had placed the book in my bedside drawer, but I needed a settled mind to read it. My pregnancy was keeping me too preoccupied. The last visit to my gynecologists had not gone as expected. The doctors suspected that the fetus was not properly forming. I was terrified and my nerves were already weakened by Mom's sudden death – now this.

Mom had always been a person of great faith, and that's what kept her moving ahead. I very rarely prayed, but amongst Mom's stuff, I found her prayer book. She had special prayers for everything. I began working frantically on my faith; my unborn child needed it. This suddenly made me realize the one obvious truth, that only God can fix everything. I knew very soon I would have to go to India to visit the shelter. I was ready to get involved. All my parents' friends who had attended my mother's funeral had such good words for the effort that Mom had put into this venture. I thought it was a brilliant idea in those days, where women were going through so much struggle and torture. Finally, there was a place where they would be sheltered. I had read many horrific stories about women in other countries who had suffered due to dowry demands, incest, and abuse, and their only escape was death.

In India it was a part of the upbringing of girls that they were taught to be quiet and never talk about their problems. This would only increase problems for the rest of the family. In a man's world, a women's mere existence was a privilege, she was fed and clothed, and that was more than she deserved. If anything went wrong in her life, she was to be blamed. There were many orphanages, but no shelters where any girl was welcome to live and be happy, no matter what had scarred her life. I remember once, Mom had called this mission, "Preservation of life." Now I understood what she meant.

During my sixth month of pregnancy, things were looking better, and the fetus was doing well. Ahmed had to travel to Egypt on business for two months, and I couldn't travel due to my pregnancy. It was very lonely after Ahmed left. I finally got the time to read Mom's book.

Now I knew who Yusuf Ali was, and what he meant to Mom. I was shocked – I could never imagine mom ever being in love, and with a heel like

Yusuf, no less. Why couldn't Mom see through him? I was angry at my mother, and couldn't understand why she had to suffer so much. I really was in a fit. I wanted to go and thrash up Yusuf's grave. Then it dawned on me that I was actually angry because Mom didn't tell me this before. Why did I never ask her about her life? It was too late; she had wasted her precious years crying for this stupid man. Mom had finished her book right up to the present time. I would only have to end it by writing her last few days. It would require me to relive her last moments, to write about them honestly. I knew my mother so much better now, but only after her death. All her life, she drifted between the turmoil of having loved and having committed this crime of not letting go of that love. It was this bitter truth that she couldn't swallow, that she had let down her father.

Sheraz called often to check on how the baby and I were doing. He would fill me up on the daily happenings at the shelter. I was so relieved that everyone in India had accepted me, as if I was Mom. I am sure Mom didn't expect this from me. You never know what life has in store for you. I had had very different plans for my life, but who was I to decide? It had been already decided for me.

Sheraz told me that his wife Fatima was expecting their first child. They wanted me to come to India for his birth. After having read Mom's book, I seemed to feel so connected to everyone. I was so happy for Fatima. I knew if I did publish Mom's book, I would have to change names and places, for obvious reasons. Little Selma was about twelve now and was doing well in a public school. Sheraz told me that sometimes she still had nightmares about her parents. Selma had grown very attached to my mom, and now with her sudden death, the poor angel had suddenly become so serious and all grown up. Fatima was trying her best to get close to her, but Sheraz felt that Selma was too scared to get attached to anyone.

I kept reading Mom's book every night I wanted to know her so well that I could write as if she was writing. Mom's book had become a little life dictionary for me, with the meaning of love, motherhood, friendship, pain, and betrayal. Mom hid this from me, so that I could form my own interpretations of life, and I had; thanks to my mom, this was totally my own life.

Every time I thought about the end of Mom's life, I would put off writing it. I would look pleadingly up into the sky and say, "Mom I don't like this ending, you know I like only happy endings."

I was due any day, and my frequent visits to the Asian market were getting tough on me. I would visit the market, park my car in the parking lot, visit every store and talk to everyone there, so that I could gather details of Mom's last moments. Everyone had such good things to say about her. Sometimes when a gentle wind touched me soulfully, I felt it was Mom. I would go and eat all the Indian junk food that Mom loved so much. In one of these stores a young boy named Prakash, who worked there, told me that he was in the parking lot when Mom had her deadly fall. Prakash gave me minute details about Mom's very last moments. I was so grateful to him, because it was only through his memory of the actual events that I was able to know and wite about Mom's death. Prakash also told me that he and some other people tried to revive her till the ambulance came. He told me that Mom's last word was "Baba." Prakash asked me if my mother called me Baba. I smiled and told him that Mom was calling out to her father, whom she lovingly called Baba.

I had been coming here for months now and every time, I would go and visit the flower market. But I wasn't able to see the champa flower; I was told that they were out of season now. Sometimes I would sit on the stairs, from where Mom fell, and would try to visually recreate how it all might have happened. By now I had quite a bit of detail about Mom's activities during those last few hours.

I knew she had ordered the food; that I had to cancel, since the wedding had been postponed. We found the sari she had bought; it is in my closet now, I hope to wear it once I'm slim again. Thanks to Prakash's narration, I could now visualize my mother's end. Reading her life story, I realized that Mom had yearned for her father's affection and forgiveness. It made sense that her last word was a call to him.

Now I realized why Mom had made Dad so important to me, and why she spoke about him to me all the time. She knew how dear fathers are to daughters. She tried her best, so that I may not have the same painful void in my life.

Two week after our daughter Sana was born, uncle Shabir passed away. He was eighty-nine. I felt very alone, I regretted being the only child. Sheraz was the last strand of my parent's family. Ahmed was back in time for my delivery. Our lives were changed overnight by the coming of a child. When Sana was about three months old, I took her to Dad and Mom's gravesite. We both sat there quietly – well, at least I did. Sana kept mumbling away. I was sure Mom was enjoying every sound she was making. The grim atmosphere of a graveyard was suddenly filled with life. I sat there for hours talking to both of my parents, telling them how I was enjoying being a mother, and that every time I would feel lost, I would refer to the little "Mom dictionary" in my heart. All my answers were always there.

It was spring now, and a lot of wild flowers were swaying in its magical winds.

Mom loved flowers, and I knew she was happy now. She was right, this didn't look like a graveyard; it looked more like "another world." Sitting there and inhaling her presence, in a moment of absolute silence when even the wind was still, I think I heard Mom whisper to me, "Lucknow." I knew how much Mom loved her homeland, but perhaps she was trying to remind me of my promise. I had promised Sheraz that I would come to India and take care of the shelter. I smiled, fondly touched their graves, and whispered back, "I'll go to India."

As I was leaving the site, a strong wind blew and I could see the dust mingle and swirl between their graves. I was sure that I had made the right decision, to bury Mom here with Dad.

Yusuf never deserved her, dead or alive. I would have made a colossal mistake if we had buried Mom in the Muslim cemetery, where Yusuf was.

Ahmed was doing a lot of traveling for his job. This gave me an opportunity to ask him if I could go to India for few months. Sheraz advised me that since it was summer in India, I should delay my trip till December, when it would be quite pleasant. That was perfect, because Sana would be six months old, and Ahmed had a two-month trip to Bangalore then. I was so excited because I had never been to India before. I would finally see Mom's motherland and get to go through Mom's history. Being an archeologist, India had always fascinated me. Just like Egypt, India was a land of hidden mysteries for me. The sands of time were taking me back, to the land of my forefathers.

25

Ahmed had to leave for Bangalore a week earlier than scheduled. Sana and I had our flight to Lucknow booked for the next Wednesday. Once I arrived at the airport in Lucknow, I had a big shock. There were too many people all around, everyone spoke too loudly, it was dirty, unorganized, and I was terrified.

It took me about three hours to get through customs. Sana was overwhelmed, and I felt as if I had stepped into a battlefield. Finally I saw a loving face looking at me, and guessed it was Sheraz.

He approached me and said, "I am Sheraz," and without any other word we hugged each other. He then remarked, "You look so much like your Mom that I could recognize you anywhere." He grabbed Sana from my arms, and covered her face with a white loincloth. There was a pretty girl with him. I assumed it was Fatima, his wife. She greeted me, and took my hand, dragging me through this sea of people in to a white ambassador car.

Sheraz explained to me that there was too much dust in the air, and it may not be good for the little baby. Fatima smiled at me, and offered me a similar piece of cloth to cover my face. Sheraz didn't want me to stay in a hotel and therefore had cleaned up a room for us, as best as he could, in his house. Women are overprotected in India. Sheraz was about six years older than me, but he doted over me like a father. I was just enjoying being with family.

Fatima and Sheraz were trying their best to keep me comfortable, but it was a drastic change of scene for me. Everything was dusty, Sana was sneezing away, and I started to get a sore throat. For the next few days, Sana and I remained confined in my room. I was scared to go out or to expose Sana any more. I had made this decision to come here, in a very emotional frame of mind, and now reality was getting hard to swallow. Both Sana and I had a fever for four days. Sheraz was really nervous; he was getting the feeling that we shouldn't have come. The first day after my fever had gone I was having a cup of tea with Fatima when she awakened my soul with a thoughtful comment.

She remarked, "This is your mother's home, she spent half of her life here. You are her daughter, her flesh and blood; how can you be uncomfortable here?" I wanted to give her a big list of reasons, but the deep truth in her statement stopped me. She held my hand and said, "Relax, enjoy, you are home now and I can bet you will be fine."

Fatima was right. By the second week of our visit Sana and I were well adjusted to our new environment, I guess because I stopped being afraid of it.

That evening, Sheraz came over to me and said, "I think you are ready now.

Let's visit the shelter, everyone is waiting eagerly to see you." As I entered, I saw a big plank that read the name of Selma as the founder and the names of many mothers as donors or caretakers. I smiled, knowing I was looking at Mom's gratitude for that one person who knew her, and loved her unconditionally. I felt a sense of warmth as if I was really in the IN THE ARMS OF A MOTHER. Everyone came and gathered around me, and I knew each of them was trying to find even a slight glimpse of my mother in me. They wanted to feel that Sharmeen Bakhtiar was back in their lives. As everyone stood chattering around me, a very beautiful thought soothed my mind: they saw my mother in me. Now I was sure she was alive in me. Suddenly I had all her enthusiasm and compassion rushing through me. Sheraz and Fatima had taken real good care of the shelter. Everything was very organized and comfortable, like home.

A sharp alarm rang, and all the girls got up, and started towards the kitchen. Sheraz said, "It's time to cook. After they come back from school or work, everyone pitches in and the meals are made."

I wanted to help too. I handed Sana to one very eagerly waiting ten-year-old, and walked into the kitchen. The girls were very hesitant. They said I didn't need to help, and that I could just watch them. I didn't want to intrude into their comfort zone yet, I was new to them, and so I talked and watched. It was so amazing; even the eight-year-old Savita was cutting vegetables and washing the plates. They were like this perfect team of elves. Savita was a very charming little girl. She had a wheat-like complexion, light brown eyes, and short dusty hair. Sheraz told me that she came into the shelter about a year ago. It seems her parents had abandoned her, as they were too poor to feed her. She was found one morning on the doorsteps of the shelter. I thought that was the saddest thing. I knew how precious children are; they are the joy of our life. Parents, who have to sacrifice everything for the betterment of their children, must possess great courage. I became very fond of Savita, and she became a good friend of my Sana.

Lucknow was finally sinking into my being. It started to give me a feeling of home. Ahmed liked India and was trying his best to get transferred to Lucknow, but it was difficult. Lucknow was not as developed as Bangalore was, and foreign companies had not yet found it profitable to invest here. Lucknow was still sleeping in its past grandeur, and I loved it. I liked that people were so content and happy, and that there wasn't such a rush to follow the progressing world. People felt that progress would come to them in time. They didn't have to run after it, and till then they should just enjoy their lives.

I started to order some educational books from England for the girls. They all seemed so eager to learn. I guess they had nothing else to worry about. Selma was now thirteen, and she was turning out to be a real beauty. One day, very late in the evening, we had a visitor. The girls were all busy cooking dinner, and Sheraz and I were discussing future plans, when a young man appeared at the door. Sheraz stared at him for few minutes, and was sure he knew him, but just couldn't place him. The man smiled and said, "I met you at your uncle's funeral. I am Asif, remember now?" Sheraz at once shook his hands, and was very pleased to meet him. I was told that this young man was an orphan whom my grandfather had taken care of. Asif, in order to make some money for his studies, used to deliver tea at my grandfather's office. My grandfather liked his dedication and sponsored his education. Asif was back in town, and thanks to my granddad, he had become a civil engineer. He told me all about his life story. I listened to his narration, as we shared a cup of Sheraz's famous chai.

Asif wanted to help the residents of shelter in whatever way he could. He felt that the time had come when he could return the favor done to him. He was very saddened by my mother's death, and praised her courage and her love for the humanity. He was so happy that through this shelter I had kept her spirit alive. I told him that I thought this shelter had given life to many destitute and helpless girls.

26

Every evening I would go for long walks with Sheraz, and he would narrate a tale about every house we passed by: who used to live there, and what happened to them. He would walk with me down to street corners where my mother had spent time. Mom's old school and the famous pipal tree, which still stood tall and mighty like a guardian of the ages. The school was renovated, and looked very fancy now; it had been turned into a private school. I had decided that if we did stay back in Lucknow forever, I would send my daughter to this school. When we passed Yusuf's house, Sheraz had a lot to say about him. It looked like Yusuf had impressed Sheraz, too, with his charms.

The more I knew about Yusuf, the more I felt bad for my mother. I was standing at a threshold, where I could see how naive and innocent my mother was, and Yusuf a fox. I wished that Mom had had someone who could have guided her and saved her. I kept muttering in my head, "Mom why, why couldn't you see through him?" Suddenly I had this very funny feeling – I was being a mother to my mother.

I wished I could have been there for her, and saved her from this worthless person.

Sheraz again broached the topic and asked, "When are you going to publish your mother's book?" I replied that I was ready for that, and would put my heart and soul into completing it.

I knew I had to change the names of characters and locations, but one thing that I was absolutely sure of was that Yusuf must not be mentioned in her book. What no one could do in her lifetime, I could do. I erased Yusuf; I erased the one mistake that my mom had made. Her slate was clean now, and I was happy.

It was so normal for a mother to hide or erase her child's mistakes; for once a child could return the favor.

But then I realized that Mom would have wanted people to read about Yusuf, so that young girls would realize the follies of the human heart, and not be blinded and call it love. Mom would have really wanted to warn other daughters and sisters to be aware of manipulating, selfish people like Yusuf Ali. Moreover, I thought that when Mom herself was setting down every event of her life, I had no right to erase it. It wouldn't be honest; after all, we learn from the mistakes of others.

However, I extended greater focus on Selma's life. I would list this story as a realistic fiction. There was Mom's reality, and then I wanted to add the stories and plight of these young girls. Mom would have wanted the world to know, so that in the future, other victims of rape and incest would have the much-needed courage to stand up against their vicious offenders.

I would write a new script of my mother's life, and it would also include the lives and stories of her dear daughters. After all, Fatima, Savita, Selma, and all the other girls had treated Mom as their own mother. Mom's mission to speak about the plight of these and many other girls had to be published.

I had a very dear friend in England, who now worked for a publishing house. I told her about my mother's life story, and that I would complete it and then add a bit of what she had left behind. It would be the story of an ordinary woman and her many daughters. Most importantly, I wanted to write what mom would have wanted to convey to the world. My friend was very eager to publish such a book, and told me to take enough time to complete the writing.

I had a very pretty picture of my mother in my wallet. I sat on my bed with Sana in my arms, and I showed her the picture and said, "Look, pretty Granma." She smiled and kissed the photo, and as I gently wiped her drolly kiss from the photo, I stared into Mom's eyes for the first time. I had never realized that Mom had the most mysterious eyes; they were kind of brown, with a few rays of grey. I started to look very closely at her picture; we never realize that sometimes all that is left behind is a captured image.

She had very soft cheekbones, and thin delicate lips. As she smiled, very faint dimples would make her face so desirable. Her long, straight hair framed and enhanced her lovely, well-chiseled face. It seemed as if God was very fond of her; she emitted a glow of innocence and goodness. There was no way one could read the struggle, the sadness, and the pain of betrayal that hid behind those loving eyes.

Ahmed by now was sure that he wanted to settle in India. We had been missing the most important part of our lives, our culture, and our roots. We were not sent down to this earth only to make money, we are supposed to live and enjoy the blessing called life. Our roots were holding us down, which is why we decided to live here, for this felt like home now, and we knew that we belonged here.

Ahmed bought a small flat in Bangalore and I bought a small flat here in Lucknow. I was enthralled. So much more could be done now that I didn't have to go back.

We started working on our future plans, to spread this shelter concept to other needy cities and small towns. I took up a part-time job at the city museum as a curator. Lucknow was filled with old palaces, huge monuments, and amazing architecture, and undiscovered history.

I had read about world history all my life, now I was getting to live it.

India is the birthplace of civilization, and thus the perfect place for an archeologist.

Asif had now become a constant handyman at our shelter. Everything that needed to be fixed was saved for Asif. He was doing pretty well at his job, and making a decent amount of money. Asif had bought a small apartment, about six miles away from the shelter. He had also invested in a second-hand scooter, which helped him to commute. Every evening after work, he would come over to the shelter, and provide whatever help he could.

One evening I was sitting outside in our now-beautiful garden, when Asif came and sat beside me. He was very nervous. After a long stream of "It's nothing," out came the burning truth. He said that if it was all right with me and Sheraz, he wanted to marry Selma. He said he knew everything about her life and wanted to heal her pain by his love. My eyes welled with tears. I hugged him, and said this was the best way he could have ever made my mother and father happy. Selma was thirteen now, and Asif was twenty-one. I thought it would be nice to get them married when she was sixteen. He agreed, and said that I should at least let him take responsibility for her from now on. I agreed. Selma didn't have the faintest idea. She was still very shy and hesitant to make any attachment. Sheraz and Fatima were very happy about Asif's proposal. They said that they would break it gently in time to Selma. We didn't want to force her into anything. Those days in Lucknow, it was very normal for girls to be married at the age of thirteen, but I wanted to give Selma some time to adjust.

We decided that we needed to go to other towns,

study the need for shelters, and open them. But we needed funds for this. Sheraz and I went to a small town called Sarangpur. It was about a two-hour train ride from Lucknow city. We stayed for nearly one week in a dingy little hotel, trying to find some lead as to who would want to fund our shelters. I think we met nearly all the well-established and rich people there, but none of them wanted to invest money where there would be no profit. The world was speeding towards progress, and so everything else could wait. I remember it was a very hot day when Sheraz and I were standing at the train station to take the train back home. We were both so tired and disappointed that we just stood there like statues, gazing into the heady air.

A man wearing a somewhat dirty kurta pajama approached us. Sheraz started to apologize to him, for he took him for a beggar. This man smiled at him and said, "You don't know me. I work at the municipal office where you two were inquiring about a place for your shelter. I'm happy I caught you in time." I at once asked him if he was in trouble and needed help. He gently placed two pieces of paper in my hand. The smaller piece had a local address written on it, and the other was a check for 45 lakhs.

Sheraz saw our train approaching, but I didn't want to leave yet. Was this man kidding with us? I had to know more. I sat with him on a nearby wooden bench and sent Sheraz to get some chai for us. This man had a very complaisant look on his face. I could see he was very frugally dressed, and his shoes were about to give way any moment.

He started to talk. "My name is Satish Shah. I used to be a very famous businessman in this town. But that all is in the past, I don't want to bother you with details, I'm in a rush. This check is real, this is my life savings," and he paused, as if it was too painful for him to utter the next statement. "My wife and my only daughter died in a plane crash. I had nothing and no one to live for, but I had so much money, and I wanted to put this money into right use. I regret that I could not save them, but this money can save other lives. I was very impressed with your concept; yes we do need a home for such girls."

The address that he gave me was that of his house, a mansion. "I waited all these years, hoping that my family would come back home, so I kept saving this money and this house for them. I never realized that this house could be home to a new family. You have given me closure. I know that these needy girls are like daughters to me, and by saving them and sheltering them, my soul will finally rest in peace."

He bid us success and goodbye, and took a train to the holy city of Banaras, where he could finally live.

Sheraz and I stood there in shock for a while. Who was this man, and was he a man or some angel sent by God? I really didn't care, I was so happy that we could spread our wings, and give shade to many more scorched souls. Sheraz was still very apprehensive; he just couldn't believe that a person could be so selfless.

The house that Satish left us was huge. We were excited, and we decided to keep the same name: "In the arms of a mother." We got the formalities and legalities taken care of. Mr. Satish had sent a legal letter to the authorities, transferring the property in the name of the shelter. Sheraz hired a security guy to take care of the house while we went back to Lucknow. There were no residents yet at this new home, but I knew the word would spread. I had left word with a lot of local social workers about the shelter.

The next morning in Lucknow, I saw that Savita, the little nine-year-old, seemed very distraught. She looked as if she was coming out of some grave sickness.

Fatima inquired, but she kept saying, "I'm fine I just feel too tired." Sheraz offered to take her to a doctor, but she refused. Savita did say that she didn't want to go to the grocery today, and Sheraz offered to go.

At dinner I noticed that Sheraz was fuming with anger. I asked Fatima if she knew the reason. She told me that she would tell me later. After dinner, as usual Fatima, Sheraz, and I sat out in the front porch to have chai. I asked Fatima again, and she started to say something when Sheraz jumped in, and started to fling curses at the grocer. What I gathered from his fuming was that the grocer and some of his friends had accused Sheraz of running a prostitution scam here under the name of a shelter. I think Sheraz got into a fistfight with the grocer, Mohan. Fatima later filled me in that Mohan was connected with some local youth group, which was funded by some corrupt politicians. Hence they would blatantly commit crimes, and the police would do nothing about it. This had become very common in all the states. During election time, the politicians needed these youth to collect funds, and sometimes force the elderly people to vote for them. I was flabbergasted. "But this is illegal," I said.

Fatima smiled and said, "Keep your eyes open, you will see it all around you." I knew Fatima had seen a very harsh side of life, which my mother had kept me unaware of. Living here with these girls, I saw and realized how difficult some people's lives are; I felt blessed. This was all very new to me. I felt I had come out of a safety bubble, I felt lost and scared. I began to worry about Sana growing up here, and for the first time I was unsure of whether I should be in India. I knew I could leave everything to Sheraz and Fatima and go back to London, even though I would feel like a coward, but risking my child's life, well that wasn't bravery, either. I had to discuss this with Ahmed. Maybe Bangalore was a better place and Sana could study there.

When I spoke to Ahmed he said, "Dear, your bubble has broken, and you have finally began to see the world in all its colors."

Now every time I stepped out into the open streets, I would throb with anxiety. Ahmed said. "Even in London there are bad people and crime, but your mom just shaded you too much."

I rebelled and said, "I think she did the right thing."

Ahmed retaliated by saying, "I don't want my

daughter to be unaware. I want her to be aware of reality, so that she can face it."

Our conversation ended with this note: "It's up to you. If you want to go back, no one will stop you, the world will still go on; it is only you who will have lost this miraculous opportunity to save lives."

I said to Ahmed, "Maybe you are right. I'm not needed here, everything is well taken care of, and I don't have to be here."

Ahmed responded, "Yah, you don't have to be here, you should *want* to be here.

Are you doing this as a charity? I thought you, like your mother, were doing this, because you cared, and wanted to be the humans we claim to be." I was too sacred and flustered, I was ready to run. There was so much work to be done for the new shelter, but I knew Sheraz would be able to manage it. I thought of not expressing my fears yet; maybe after the other shelter was set, it would be easy for these girls to let me go. I had realized I wasn't equipped to be my mother. These girls had become very attached to me, and I too had got quite involved in their lives. Tannu was the first girl from our shelter to finish her schooling. She wanted to go to college, and do a part time job. Sheraz didn't like the idea, as he was too scared for her. Tannu's life had been dismantled by her uncle, who molested her and was forcing her into prostitution. She fled one day from that hell, and took refuge here. Sheraz was scared, because the uncle had spotted her and had threatened Sheraz to force her to leave with him. Unfortunately, this bad man was also connected with some politician's group, and was from a well-known rich family. Tannu had refused many times to go back home. Her mother had died when she was eleven. Then her father, who was a landlord with some acres of land, suffered a stroke, and was paralyzed from the chest down. This uncle, who was her father's real brother, got into the house under the pretense of taking care of business and his brother, but his intentions were far from good.

I had a brilliant idea. I called one of my mother's friends in London, and asked her if she could sponsor Tannu, so that she could study there in London. Mrs. Bakshi not only agreed to sponsor, but she decided to pay all of Tannu's fees, too. Mrs. Bakshi was a Parsi widow, but she held a very prominent position at the Indian consulate in London. Mrs. Bakshi had spoken to many of her other Indian friends there and told them about this shelter. Six women called me and asked if they could sponsor a girl for her education there. What could be better than giving these girls the power of education? It all was so amazing, things were just falling into place.

We were not aware that Sheraz was going through a tough time with these hooligans outside. They were making his life miserable. Every time someone tries to do some good, people try to find faults with him, as if human beings are not capable of goodness. Sheraz had rented more than half of Mamu's house, so that he and Fatima could have their own income, and spend all their time with the shelter. Sheraz's little boy was growing up, he was six now. Sana and he got along very well.

It was time for Sana to start kindergarten, so I got her admitted in Mom's school. I convinced Sheraz to put his son Abid in the same school.

On the day both the kids started school, we were so happy. Sheraz was jubilant with pride and happiness. As we were leaving the school, a guy, who looked quite rough and unpolished, came up to Sheraz and said, "You have a gift waiting for you. You guys are not wanted here, close the shelter and get out, before…," then he gave us the most obnoxious snigger and walked away. Sheraz and Fatima both looked flustered, they didn't know what to expect. We sped to the shelter, but all the girls were fine, nothing was wrong or out of place.

I told Sheraz, "It was a blind bluff, don't worry." A little while later, just when we were settling down, we received a phone call. Sheraz was in shock; he wouldn't tell us anything, and dashed out of the shelter. Late that night when Sheraz finally returned, he appeared as if he had aged, his clothes were very dirty, and his face looked as if he had lost all hope and desire to live. The kids were back from school, so we knew it wasn't about them. He just dragged his feet to a bed and fell flop. Fatima was very terrified and worried for him. I told her to let him sleep. We would ask him in the morning. That whole night Fatima sat next to Sheraz's bed on the floor, holding his lifeless hand.

Early next morning, the doorbell woke us up. Fatima opened the door to find a priest from the mosque. We invited him in. He asked for Sheraz, who he said had called him here, so that they could go to the graveyard and offer special prayers for his father. Fatima and I were confused. It wasn't his death anniversary, or any religious day, so why today? The priest realized that we were not aware of last night's happenings.

The priest exhaled a deep sigh and said, "We saw the devil last night."

Then he elaborated that some of these hooligans had called Sheraz last night to the graveyard. By the time Sheraz got there, they had dug up his father's grave and scattered his remains all over very disrespectfully. They told him that the next time it would be him. They crushed his father's remains, dancing and stepping on them. It was the most evil vision Sheraz or I had ever seen. After they left, Sheraz and the priest spent hours gathering his father's remains and placing them back in his grave. This morning, Sheraz wanted special prayers to be said, to bring peace and God's grace to the departed soul.

Sheraz had heard the doorbell. He came out of his room, with the traces of last night still on his face and clothes. He told the priest to wait as he took a quick bath and put on clean clothes. Fatima and I sat with the priest, offered him tea and cookies; he looked very flustered. Fatima knew that this priest did not know Sheraz's father, yet he was torn apart over this diabolic act. He kept repeating some verses from the holy Quran as if to ward off the evil he had actually seen last night.

Sheraz came out from his room, now very well composed and calm, as if he had washed off all his distress. After the priest and Sheraz left for the graveyard, Fatima and I just looked blankly at each other, and walked our separate ways to the shelter. We were not scared, but ashamed at the reality that some human beings could stoop to this level. I sat on one of the beds quietly, and tears began to blur Sheraz's face in my eyes. Fatima just stood there at the kitchen window, waiting for Sheraz to return.

27

Next morning when I came to the shelter from my apartment, there was too much noise, as if someone was building something. All the girls were awake pretty early, and they complained about this noise. When I went into the backyard, to locate where the noise seemed to be coming from, I saw Savita, surrounded with a lot of wood. It was Sheraz who was hammering the wood pieces together and constructing something.

Fatima told me that he bought a pigeon for Savita and a special white and black pigeon for Sana. He was constructing a coop for them. Sana was so excited to see the pigeon. It reminded me of Mom's snow-white pigeon, Lucky. It felt so nice to see these two little girls shining in glee, and clinging to Sheraz's legs. Sheraz picked them up in his arms and twirled them around; the sounds of their giggles made Sheraz smile too.

This kept Sheraz busy the whole day, and let him avoid conversation. At night, when it was too dark to keep working any more, Sheraz sat down on the patio steps. I was in the kitchen just behind him. I saw Fatima go and sit next to him. They were both quiet for a while, and Sheraz kept looking up at the sky. Fatima asked him, "What are you trying to find up there?"

Without moving his gaze he said, "My father. I know he is looking at me, I feel I let him down." He told Fatima that he built this pigeon coop because his father had loved pigeons. Sheraz had wanted to have a coop here for a while and today was finally the right time to build it.

Sheraz looked at Fatima with beseeching eyes and said, "I know you feel that I should have killed those boys, or at least thrashed them up, but I cannot be like them. I prefer being killed than having to kill anyone. What is done, is done. I wish I could have stopped them from doing this, but I couldn't. To kill the evil that was burning me from inside, I chose to do something my father did every time I was hurt. He would take me to the pigeons, and let me play with them, and the innocence and purity of these birds would wipe away my pain and anger. I couldn't save my father, but I did save the goodness he had instilled in me." Fatima was still upset, she thought that Sheraz should go to the police and get them arrested. Sheraz smiled at her and said, "Do you think that would make a difference to them? They are connected with people in power." Sheraz thought that complaining to the police would aggravate their hate, and that the best way to stop hate is to stop hating.

I was listening to the whole debate, but couldn't figure out who was right. I knew people like Sheraz are considered cowards in our world, but somewhere in my heart a question arose, "Can we stop this evil?" According to Sheraz, one should protect oneself and be wise, rather than becoming that which we hate. The next day, I saw Sheraz rush into the storeroom of the shelter. He was hiding something in his hands. Fatima and I followed him. When we confronted him, he showed us a revolver, then he hid it behind the grain bags. Sheraz made us promise that none of the girls should know about this, and both Fatima and I should be aware that if need arose we would have to use the gun. This was Sheraz's way of taking precautions and being alert. It didn't make any sense to me – I had always been uncomfortable with guns, but right now it did make me feel protected.

Later that evening, Ahmed called and said that he would be joining us in Lucknow for three weeks. His flight was to arrive the next morning. I was so relieved; I missed him immensely, especially in these troubled times, I needed his hugs and comforting which always gave me strength to move on. Everyone in the shelter was very happy too, since Ahmed had become a part of their lives as well.

Seema, one of the older girls, was very good at making rice pudding or *kheer*, which Ahmed loved. Seema at once sent Savita to get some sugar from the grocer.

It was around 8:30 pm, and we were all engrossed with cleaning up the shelter and arranging good food for Ahmed. At round 10:30 pm we noticed that Savita hadn't returned. Sheraz was very upset, over why Savita was out so late. We had received an international call an hour ago which had distracted me. The call was from New Zealand, from a lady called Mrs. Dave. She had known my mother from their school days, and they had been in touch in London. Mrs. Dave's family was involved in Diamond marketing, and they were very wealthy. The couple was really blessed with every luxury of life, except a child. She had called me earlier and had expressed her desire to adopt a child from our shelter. About six months ago Mrs. Dave had come to Lucknow on a short visit. When she came to our shelter to hand us a generous check for funds, she was very attracted to Savita.

Since then she was taking care of the adoption papers and formalities. She had called today to let us know that she was arriving the next morning, and had a visa ready for Savita. Right then Savita walked in with a small packet of sugar.

Seema yelled at her, "Why are you so late?" Savita looked very tired and frazzled, and told Seema that she was in the backyard playing with the pigeons, and she forgot to bring in the sugar. Fatima came and stopped Seema from yelling, she told her to go and complete her dessert. Savita walked into her room like a zombie, and I saw Fatima staring at her with very knowing eyes. She went inside and asked Savita to have a wash and come out and eat her dinner. Savita said that she was too tired and just wanted to sleep. This wasn't the first time that Savita had behaved like this – a nine year old not hungry, that's always strange. I asked Fatima if Savita was sick. She just looked very plainly into my eyes, as if she knew what was wrong and that I wouldn't understand. She said, "She'll be fine," and walked away to her room.

Fatima wished that Sheela, the counselor that my mother had hired, was still here. Sheela had to move to Jaipur, due to her husband's job being transferred to the Jaipur office. She had really helped these girls grow. Sheraz had placed an advertisement in the local newspaper for a counselor, but no one had responded yet.

Next morning, I went to the airport to receive Ahmed and Mrs. Dave. Sheraz had accompanied me, since they were both arriving at different airports. Sana was enthralled to see her dear "Dado," – that's what she called her father.

Ahmed in return called her "Pari," meaning little fairy. Sheraz drove Mrs. Dave to the shelter, and Ahmed and I took a cab back. It was a fun-filled day. Ahmed spent the whole day chatting with the girls, and giving them gifts that he had brought for them. One of Ahmed's clients in Bangalore was a textile exporter. He had given Ahmed a whole lot of fabric for the girls, as donation for the shelter. The girls just loved the fabric; it wasn't often that they got to make new clothes, all they had was hand me downs. Ahmed and I had not realized that this would give them so much joy, for normal people sewing new clothes was so common. I told Ahmed that I was sure his client had sent this fabric with genuine feelings of goodness; hence his gift had given these girls real happiness that would last for days or maybe even years.

That evening, Ahmed announced that no dinner would be cooked at the shelter today and that he was going to take all of us out for dinner to his favorite place.

Our stomachs were churning with the mystery of where were we going.

As we drove, Ahmed kept passing by all the good restaurants. Finally the van stopped, and all the girls yelled in glee: it was their favorite kabob place, Tunda Kabobs. My Mom had told us so much about this place that we visited and relished it a lot. The one-handed guy who had started this restaurant had passed away a while ago; now this place and many more new branches were run by his sons and nephews. No matter how long it had been, the kabobs were still as mouthwatering and spicy as ever. The benches had attached tables now, but people still didn't mind eating on the street corners, it was the Lucknow lifestyle. Many big decisions were still made on these wooden benches over a cup of steaming chai and a plate of Tunda's kabobs, on a street corner. I loved this carefree lifestyle. After overloading ourselves with food, the girls still had room for ice cream or *kulfi*.

Ahmed indulged them, he smiled at my surprised face and said, "They live only in today, for their tomorrow seems so bleak to them."

I could see those colorful lights still decorating and bringing to life every street corner. I thought of Mom then, how she too might have sat on these same benches with her dad. My dad did not come to India often, but right now I was visualizing Mom and Dad sitting on one of the benches next to me.

Ahmed put his arms around my shoulders and whispered, "Thinking of Mom!" As we waited for Sheraz to bring the van around, I could still picture her, standing there looking at those colorful lights, and for a moment I felt as though she turned around and smiled at me.

Suddenly a loud commotion broke my spell. Ahmed was arguing with an old man. I had never seen him so upset. When I walked in closer some of the girls told me that this was Savita's distant uncle, who had spotted her, and was trying to drag her away. Ahmed had spotted this at the right time, and grabbed Savita back from his cruel hands.

The old uncle started to call for people, yelling loudly that Savita was his niece and that we had kidnapped her. Suddenly every stranger got involved and wanted to save Savita. Luckily Mrs. Dave, who had accompanied us for dinner, pushed through the crowd and told everyone that Savita was her daughter now. She said that this man had abandoned this little girl after her father's death, and that she had been legally adopted. Mrs. Dave showed some very concerned citizens her legal papers; I don't know if they could read, but seeing a legal seal was enough for them. After the crowd was content that no fraud was being done, they all went back to their evening activities. Mrs. Dave then walked up to that old man, and whispered something in his ears. His face flushed with every color that fear could churn. We don't know what she told him, but money has a lot of power. Mrs. Dave had a lot of it, and for once it was being used for a good cause. On our way back home, everyone looked at Mrs. Dave with awe.

Ahmed smiled at me and said, "If women stood up for each other, this world wouldn't be called a man's world, but our world."

I told Ahmed, "Yeah you are right, but you see, she has a lot of power and influence, which gives her strength and freedom."

Ahmed laughed out loud and said, "My dear, I thought strength comes from within, you just have to be aware of it and use it. We are God's greatest creations and none of us are weak."

Sheraz and I were very nervous. We asked Savita if she knew that man, and was he really her uncle? Savita had no recollection, maybe it was this man who did not want to take responsibility of a little girl, and hence he had left her on our doorstep. Mrs. Dave assured us that nothing would go wrong, that we worry too much. I guess she was too used to taking care of big ventures and getting her way, nothing bothered her. She knew that man was just here to make some money.

After this dinner incident, Savita started to trust Mrs. Dave; she became her superwoman. They would spend many hours chatting and shopping.

Mrs. Dave would always tell me, "I wish one day I can wipe away the scars that life has left on her face, and that one day she could really live." There was a deep-rooted fear that seemed to linger on Savita's face all the time.

Next morning we were all sitting down for breakfast, when Savita's uncle appeared at our doorstep. He was accompanied by a police constable. The constable asked about Savita. Fatima at once took hold of Savita's hand and sneaked her into the storeroom. Mrs. Dave and Ahmed spoke to the officer, who looked as if he had been drinking; his eyes were bloody and his legs seemed very restless. Mrs. Dave sensed that this old man had bribed the constable, and brought him here to pinch some money from us. She asked them to wait. She went inside and called the police station, asked the Sub-inspector to arrive at the shelter as soon as he could. When inspector Suresh Advani arrived, the constable, who could hardly stand on his feet and was resting on the steps, didn't even have the presence of mind to greet his superior. Inspector Suresh yanked him by his collar, and asked him why he was there and why was he in this state. It seemed this constable had been recently dismissed from the force due to misconduct. As soon as the cat was out, the mice did run away. Mrs. Dave then launched a formal police complaint against Savita's uncle.

Savita's visa and paperwork was finalized, and the flight to New Zealand was in a week. Everyone in the shelter was very happy for Savita.

Tannu's visa and sponsorship for a school in London had arrived, too. Her flight was next Wednesday. I felt as if my birds were ready to fly from their coop and that felt good. Selma was all grown up, too. Last night Asif had come over to talk about their marriage, but we were out for dinner, so he had left a note. Selma had really become a well-sculpted person and had now a lot of poise and grace. Every time I saw her, she would remind me of Mom's friend Selma, to whom Mom had dedicated this shelter. Following Mom's wishes, the new shelter was also dedicated to Selma. I knew Mom would have been so happy to see little Selma getting married. It was another dream of hers that I would be fulfilling.

That afternoon, as we waited for Asif, I sat alone in the front yard under the pipal tree. I kept going back to Mom's book and her love for her friend Selma. How Selma had saved my mother, and how her life had been full of pain. She had left this world too soon; I guess she felt she had no hope. I wish someone had opened a shelter like this then, so that Selma would be alive. I inhaled the pride I felt for my mother, for her brilliant idea for preservation of life. Sitting there, thinking of the amazing life of two dear friends, I decided that little Selma's marriage would take place in this shelter. We would send her off to a brand new life from under this very roof that had sheltered her as she healed.

Asif was renting a small flat nearby. He had a steady job now. He worked as a civil engineer with the department for road construction. He had turned out to be a very good human being. I guess goodness had touched his soul when he really needed it, and he had bloomed. He was an above average, handsome-looking fair-skinned young man. Asif never knew his parents, but seeing him now, one could assume that he had come from a good bloodline. He could have married any girl from a good family, but he was one of those crazy few who liked to return the goodness done to them. I remember that during one of our casual chats, he had told me that he was always amazed that my grandfather chose him. There were many other orphans who were as needy as he was; he was not special. He said he realized over the years that he was chosen not because of himself, but because Mr. Kazi was a good man and he just needed to shower his blessings on someone. I realized what Asif had said – he wasn't special, but grandfather was, and Asif wanted to be more like him. I started believing that "Goodness does inspire goodness."

I too wanted to use my life, my blessings, for someone who needed them. Asif continued to enlighten me. He said that when he saw Selma for the first time, he too had a moment like my grandfather; his heart just chose her.

"I guess," Asif said, "your grandfather never realized that his fleeting moment of compassion and goodness would change my life."

Asif believed that goodness was a very powerful thing, able to change someone's life, to save him. That, according to Asif, should be the first instinct of a human being. Asif was very excited, as he was now capable of taking care of Selma, fulfilling her wishes, caring for her, loving her, most of all protecting her. I was really in awe of Asif. I hoped that there could be more human beings like him and that goodness would survive in this world. Ahmed came in and both interrupted and confirmed my thoughts – he too was an amazing human being. It is true that where there is good, there is evil, but recently the scale had been very off-balance.

Selma walked in and began to show me the very gorgeous wedding dress that Asif had bought for her.

It was a deep maroon silk fabric, with rich gold thread embroidery all over it. It was gorgeous, but with all the work done on it, it did weigh a ton. Selma was so frail and petite, and she complained it was too much for her dainty body to carry this pompous attire. Fatima convinced her that since most of the time during the wedding ceremony she would be sitting down, it should be fine. Fatima mothered all these girls, and they all looked up to her for help and consultation. Selma was convinced, and Fatima's final word had reined. What really amazed me was when I was thirteen, I was so childish, but girls here seemed so mature, emotionally as well as mentally, at a very tender age.

Early marriages for girls in India were very common, and legal. Parents in this area of the world had many kids, so they were always in a rush to get their daughters married early. There were families in some parts of India where a female child was not welcome, and most of them were mercilessly killed at birth. I guess Selma had survived because she was the only child. If one belonged to a poor family and was a female child, one had a much-diminished chance to live. I knew this little girl was very special to my mother because she was the reason or the inspiration for starting this shelter. I wanted to do something special for her, since my mom was responsible for saving her and giving her a second chance to live. No doubt she was like her daughter now. I decided that I would give Mom's favorite dresser to Selma, as a wedding gift from my mother.

Sheraz, as promised, got a whole load of wood and accessories to build all the furniture for Selma's new home. Sheraz went along with Asif and Selma to check out their new abode, and take some measurements.

It was a very humble residence, a small one-bedroom flat with a very small kitchen, and a smaller bathroom. Selma still loved the place, because it was on the eighth floor, and had an amazing view of the city. Sheraz was so happy and excited and wanted every detail of Selma's wishes to be put into every piece of this house. He would sit for hours talking to her, showing her furniture designs drawn by his friend. Fatima would always push in her practical suggestions, but Sheraz was only interested in Selma's fantasies. For Sheraz, these girls had become like daughters and sisters to him, his chosen extended family. Fatima felt that Sheraz always missed having siblings and family. This brought to my attention that when Ahmed and I were gone, our only child Sana would be alone in this world. I was alone, too. I missed having a sister at least. Mom's death had come too soon, but then who can ever predict life?

Next day, I asked Sheraz to move Mom's dresser from my apartment to Selma's flat. Selma very graciously disagreed with me. I told her that she was like a daughter to my mother, and that she should have a piece of her life with her. Selma explained that instead of taking the dresser to her flat, she would prefer it to be at the shelter; after all, as she said, all the girls looked up to Sharmeen Bakhtiar as their mother and savior. Sheraz agreed, and I felt very ashamed, as I had been hoarding all my mom's belongings.

So since this house itself was the place where my mother lived and grew up, why not make it come alive by bringing all her things there, as if she had never left. The next day Sheraz and Ahmed hired some help, and moved all of Mom's furniture back where it came from.

As Sheraz was assembling the dresser mirror, all the girls gathered around, and giggled as they saw their reflection. Sheraz smiled at me and said, "Somewhere in the layers of this mirror, an image of your mother was captured, and today it also holds the image of her daughters."

Fatima cut in to add, "I'm sure she can see them now, and see their happiness through this piece of glass."

Mrs. Dave received a phone call from the New Zealand consulate informing her that some more papers would be required if Savita was to accompany her as an adopted daughter. Mrs. Dave was a very rich lady, and childless. Many of her husband's relatives didn't like the idea of this adoption. After all, they wouldn't want all her wealth being inherited by this orphan girl. So they were creating some legal hassles, but they didn't know how determined Mrs. Dave was. Mrs. Dave assured us that Savita's departure could be delayed, but not canceled. Visiting the government office here in India was a total waste of time, and always made one feel frustrated and like a fool. Some walls you just can't break, even though they serve no purpose, except the purpose of collecting more bribes from helpless and desperate civilians.

Fatima acted as Mrs. Dave's city guide, and would run around with her to the various city offices as needed. The rest of us were happily involved in the wedding preparations. Selma's wedding was not only a new start of hope for her, but it gave hope to the rest of the girls, too. They saw the light at the end of their tunnel. They hoped freely now, and breathed wishes about their own weddings. Tannu's paperwork was all done, and she would be taking her flight to London on Wednesday.

It was Monday and we had exactly one week to complete the wedding shopping and preparations. There wouldn't be any guest list, since it was just us and a few friends of Asif and Sheraz. The girls and I went to the market and bought some balloons and streamers to decorate the front lawn. Sheraz arranged for the Kazi, the priest who would be conducting the marriage, or *Nikah*. The food for the wedding day would be cooked by all of us. It would be a simple occasion, and the girls were ok with it; what mattered was that they would get married and have a life. There was a lot of noise and happy commotion going about the shelter. In the back yard, Sheraz and his friend Kasim hurried to finish the furniture, as they had only three days and they would need one day to set up the furniture in the flat. Selma was upset since she couldn't take the pigeons with her; we told her that the pigeons would give her a reason to come and see her sisters at the shelter. Ahmed's contribution for the wedding was kabobs and kulfi for everyone, a yummy gift.

Two days to the wedding, and Mrs. Dave was already pulling her hair apart. She couldn't believe how lazy and corrupt some government officers could be. Savita's paper work was taking too much time, or as Mrs. Dave put it, nothing really moves here. Well, what people forget is that in so many years, our country *has* moved, has gotten better, but our pace is a little slow.

As I've mentioned before, here in Lucknow, people loved to take their own sweet time. They enjoyed every moment; work came second, and fun came first.

The lunch hours would very easily be stretched from thirty minutes, to two hours. People who lived close by went home, had lunch, took a short siesta, and just reappeared at work. It is very hot in Lucknow, so people hated working during the noon hours, and low-budget offices didn't have air-conditioning. They had very low salaries, and that's how the inclination to take bribes was infested. One had to bribe or tip all the officers, including the office clerk or coffee boy. It was frustrating, but there was no other way to motivate them.

The wedding day had arrived. Selma was drenched

with the reality that she would have to leave her shelter, and fly into the open sky. She wanted to cry, she thought of her mother, and then she didn't want to think about the last memory of her parents. She had wiped off her past; all she could think of was sitting on these steps and talking to Sharmeen. Today she finally grasped how much Sharmeen and this shelter had done for her. Selma was happy now; she was getting the new start that she wanted.

At 6 pm, Sheraz arrived at the shelter with the priest. We all were gathered happily but solemnly on the front porch. Fatima and the girls had laid down fresh bed sheets on the floor, and we all sat on them. Kazi Riaz started to read from the Quran, some verses that were to be recited for a wedding ceremony. Our heads were covered with scarves in respect. Then the priest asked Selma three times if she was willing to accept Asif as her husband. On the third and final call, Selma very shyly and meekly replied, "Yes." After the girl gave her consent and acceptance, the priest then asked Asif for his consent to this marriage and acceptance of Selma as his lawful wife. The marriage was complete and solemnized. Everyone clapped with joy. Fatima and Sheraz were the first to bless the newlyweds. Sheraz became very emotional. Fatima smiled and told me that Sheraz had cried even at his own wedding ceremony. This was his unique way of healing or letting go. Sheraz didn't bother about our comments; he lovingly took Selma aside, and spoke to her about her rights and obligations as a wife and the new path she was about to tread. He then very affectionately handed her an envelope. It contained his savings, about three thousand rupees. He told Asif and Selma that this would help them in starting their new life. Asif very humbly refused to take the money. He said that Sheraz had already done enough for them, and that it was now his responsibility to take care of Selma.

Selma realized how much Fatima and Sheraz loved her. She hugged Fatima very dearly and wept on her shoulders.

Fatima wiped her tears and said, "From now on no more tears, only happiness shall dwell on this face."

Selma was feeling as if all this was a dream. She had never expected that marriage and happiness were written in her destiny. As Selma was leaving, she turned for the last time to look at the shelter, and then she looked straight into Asif's loving eyes and said, "Today I have witnessed Gods mercy."

Asif smiled back at her, and said, "And me too."

Sheraz wanted this marriage to take place in a very humble but traditional way. He had rented a horse-driven tanga to send the newlywed couple off to their home. We all were so surprised, none of us had considered this thoughtful little detail. We had all expected that Ahmed would drop them off in his car. The carriage was decorated with twinkling lights and fresh flowers. The tanga driver was Jabbar, a friend of Sheraz who rented his tanga for wedding ceremonies to make some extra money. Sheraz brought his friend in, and asked him to have dinner with everyone. After dinner, we all got Selma ready for her new journey. Asif was bubbling with joy, and that put Selma at ease. She hugged us all, and we all said our farewells. Sheraz settled the couple comfortably in the tanga. Jabbar, the tanga driver, came towards me and handed me a package covered with banana leaves. "This is for you" he said. "You don't know me, but I knew your grandparents and your mother. I am Baban's son. My father used to work for your family." I was shocked and delighted.

I told him I knew about his father as told by my mom. I opened the package, it had some special type of flowers inside. They were very fragrant, with very delicate stems, white in color with a thin yellow outline.

Jabbar smiled at me and said, "Your grandmother and mother loved these flowers, these are champa flowers." Jabbar related that he and his late sister Raffia enjoyed coming to this house with their father, and that my mother and grandmother have done a lot for his family. Every time he would see these flowers, it made him think of their kindness. "May God bless their souls," he prayed. I felt as if I knew this man already. I had read about him, and now I could see him in reality. Sheraz told me that Jabbar was doing pretty well, driving the tanga as his father had done.

Selma left, and even though there were still many of us in the shelter, it felt so empty. We sat in the veranda till very late that night. Everyone was too chirpy to sleep. Sheraz was telling me about Jabbar, how he had started with one rickshaw, and now he owns seven. He has hired drivers who gave him rent for using his rickshaws to earn a living. But I kept thinking of Jabbar's elder sister Raffia, who had hung herself so that her family's life could be better.

I wondered if Jabbar knew about his sister's sacrifice.

Mrs. Dave was grumbling about the last paper

that she needed to complete for Savita's sponsorship. She had been promised by some high official, whom she had compensated handsomely, that she was to get the legal document next Monday. Mrs. Dave told Sheraz that tomorrow they should call the travel agent and get the tickets set for next Tuesday. Sheraz was hopeful, but knowing the unpredictable nature of government offices, he told Mrs. Dave to wait till she actually had the paper in her hand. Booking the ticket would not be a problem. Mrs. Dave just threw her hands helplessly into the air, and decided to call it a day. We all started to wind up and move back to our rooms.

28

FATIMA

Next morning every one woke up late. Nazneen, who had been working hard on painting her flower pots, was pleading with Sheraz to go with her to the market place to sell her creations. All the girls did what they wanted. We saw to it that first they complete their basic education, and after that, like any normal daughters, they were allowed to follow their dreams. Everyone was free to choose the hobby of her choice or talent, and we never forced anyone to do handicrafts or carpentry work to make money for the shelter. This was their home, and we were their parents. Whatever money they did make, they were expected to keep it for themselves.

Some of the girls had saved a small fortune, and now they were happy that they had done so, hoping that one day they, too, would get married and have a home of their own.

All the maintenance and food was managed by donors. We had not brought these girls here so that they could work for us; we brought them here so that they could have a home.

One of the eldest girls here, Gopi, who had just finished her education, had taken up a job at a local government office. Gopi had been from a well-to-do family, but she had suffered incest in her joint family. Gopi knew that she had to leave her home if she wanted to protect herself. Her mother was helpless and weak; she did not have the courage to stand up for her daughter. Gopi was the only daughter among four brothers. No one ever came looking for her. We all were very proud of Gopi.

It was late that afternoon, and breakfast had turned into brunch since we all woke up so late. We all were dragging our heels with the cleaning. Fatima was cleaning up the mess the girls had made in the kitchen, making *parathas*.

While washing the dishes, she gazed out of the window into the back yard. She could see all the pigeons happily chirping and eating their breakfast. Fatima noticed that Savita was not in the backyard. She had heard Savita wake up pretty early as she normally did, because she liked to be the one to feed the pigeons in the morning. Savita had been playing all morning at the pigeon pen. Fatima had heard her laughing and talking to the birds, when other girls were busy with their brunch. Around 2 pm, Fatima went into the back yard to get a clearer view. Savita was nowhere to be seen. No one had sent her on any errand, so where could she have gone? Fatima questioned all the girls. Sheraz sipped calmly on his hot chai and told Fatima not to worry. I too thought that she might have walked to some neighbor's house and was telling her never-ending stories. Fatima stared at all of us as she sensed a lingering silence in the shelter. She became restless; she wiped the sweat form her face, and told Sheraz that she was going out to look for Savita.

Late afternoons during summer months are usually very hot, and the wind blows gusts of heat. During these times the streets are lonely and abandoned. The tar road was burning hot. Fatima could feel the heat seeping through her rubber slippers. It felt as if she was walking on hot coal. The rubber on her slippers was sticking to the street. She shaded her eyes with her hands, and tried to look through the haze. "Where could she have gone in this heat?" she muttered to herself, reaching the first house that

Savita liked to visit. There was no one at home. Fatima walked to every house, but no one had seen Savita since this morning. After an hour or so, Fatima returned, disturbed by her search. She asked for Sheraz, I told her that he was with his pigeons. Fatima went out back to find him. Sheraz was standing near the gate of the back fence. He looked confused, and was inspecting the gate very closely. Fatima rushed to him, and informed him that Savita could not be found. She was angry that instead of paying attention to her fears, he kept looking at the broken gate. After a great deal of nervous nagging from Fatima, Sheraz finally stood up, and looked at Fatima with utmost fear in his eyes. He haplessly showed Fatima a broken piece of a lock, and said, "I think someone broke into the back yard." They both knew what that implied; they both refused to believe in the fear that screamed through their eye. They held each other's hand and rushed into the shelter.

Sheraz at once took control. Determining that Mrs. Dave was the most affected by the loss, he asked her to go to the police station and report Savita missing.

Sheraz looked at Fatima and said that she should take me and go look for Savita at the park, or the market. Fatima asked what he was planning to do. Sheraz said, "I have to look for her at a certain place, pray that my fears don't come true."

Fatima pressed his hands with deep-felt love and said, "We will all pray, go find her."

Somewhere in her heart, Fatima knew where Sheraz was going.

Fatima and I scanned each and every possible place. The sky looked grey and scary, a big storm was approaching. Before we knew it, the clouds got darker, and swift winds started to blow across the sky. Everyone started to take shelter and close their shops. In a few minute the whole marketplace looked like an abandoned town. I told Fatima that we should head back to the shelter; maybe Sheraz had found Savita.

Sheraz walked fearfully to the grocery store. Mohan's friend Raju was on the counter, and he was getting ready to pull the shutters down, to close the store before the storm. Sheraz approached him and asked Raju if Savita had come here. Raju had a very desperate and guilty look on his face. Sheraz's question had scared him; he nervously pushed Sheraz out of the store, and said, "Get going, I have to close the store. Mohan is not here, and I don't know anything about this girl you speak about." Raju pulled the shutters down loudly and left Sheraz to face the approaching storm.

Sheraz could hardly walk back, the wind was pushing him too hard, but there was a bigger storm that was churning his mind and making him weak. The girls had begun to close all the doors and windows of the shelter. Sheraz, Fatima, and I, we all reached the shelter gate at the same time. The sun was a furious red, and the wind was destructive – all of nature was fearful of what was to come. Suddenly, within few minutes, the wind became mild, and the sun hid behind the deep clouds: it rained for the first time in nearly a year. We were all watching this fearful dance of nature hiding behind our own clouds, but Sheraz refused to come in.

He wanted to get battered by the storm, as a way of punishing himself.

He sat there in the front porch, getting drenched, and his eyes were fixed in a never-wavering stare at the gate.

After the storm passed, we all came out and sat under the porch with Sheraz.

At around 8:30 pm we saw Savita walk in through the gate. Sheraz ran and hugged her. Savita collapsed, and Fatima and I ran to gather her in our arms. We took her into her bedroom, and everyone followed us in. As Fatima laid Savita on her bed, she noticed that the lower portion of Savita's dress was soaked in blood. She stared at me, and frantically asked everyone to leave the room. She told Sheraz that he needed to go and get an ambulance; we would have to take Savita to the hospital. As Fatima started to close the bedroom door, she pulled me inside, and told everyone else that we had to give Savita a wash before we took her to the hospital. Fatima and I took Savita to the bathroom. She was going in and out of consciousness. We made her rest on the bathroom chair, and Fatima began to splash water on her face.

For quite some time, Savita was too feeble even to talk, and as she gained consciousness, she clung to Fatima and began to sob. Fatima gently caressed her tangled hair and whispered to her, "Don't worry, you will be fine. It's all over now, you are safe." We gave her a bath; I ran and brought some cookies from the kitchen. Savita gobbled them feverishly. After Fatima had dressed her in clean clothes, she told Savita very lovingly, "Don't be afraid; just tell me the name of the person who hurt you." I moved away, I knew Savita was not that comfortable with me yet, but Fatima had been a mother to her. After a lot of coaxing, Savita helplessly whispered something in Fatima's ears. Fatima stared at me in horrific disbelief, and Savita lost consciousness again.

Sheraz knocked at our door and informed us that the ambulance had arrived. Fatima opened the door, and she looked as if she was in a trance. She just stood there. Sheraz entered the room and carried Savita to the ambulance. He asked me to stay back with the girls, and said that Mrs. Dave would accompany them in the ambulance. Sheraz called out to Fatima, asked her to get into the ambulance soon. Fatima walked up to him lifelessly, caught his hand, and said, "You and Mrs. Dave go ahead. I have something very important to take care of, I'll be there soon." Sheraz didn't have the inclination to ask her what could be more important than this, so he left with Savita.

As Fatima stood on the street watching the ambulance leave, Savita's pain-filled voice echoed in her ears: "It was Mohan, Raju, Ravi, and Salman." Savita, a nine-year-old girl, had been gang raped. Fatima couldn't understand how Savita was still alive. Every nerve in her body was trembling with the urge to destroy the wrong-doers. What bothered Fatima most was why she couldn't have seen this coming. She had worried that Savita was in some kind of trouble, but she couldn't read in her innocent eyes the fear of the oncoming storm.

After about an hour of standing outside in the darkness, and just aimlessly pacing up and down the street, Fatima came in and went straight to the storeroom. She came out after few seconds, and informed me that she was leaving for the hospital. I asked her, "What was the important thing that you needed to do?" She smiled at me and said, "I will do that before I go to the hospital. Take care of the girls."

Fatima went straight to Mohan's grocery store. Raju was at the counter; she grabbed him by his collar and started to beat him ferociously.

Mohan, who was inside, heard the racket and came out. By now they had guessed that Fatima knew of their crime, but to them she was neither a human being nor someone to whom they had to answer. All four men grabbed her and pulled her into the back of the store. Mohan directed Raju to shut the shutters. They sniggered at her helpless plight, and tried to be disrespectful to her. She was just few pounds of flesh for them. They hammered her black and bloody red, and Mohan joked about raping her, too. Fatima regained her strength, and pulled out the revolver that she had brought from the shelter.

Raju tricked her and grabbed the gun from her. That's when Mohan interrupted with the suggestion that Salman should lock her up in the toilet. Mohan wanted to be sure that no one else knew of their crime.

There was a crack in the wooden door of the toilet. Fatima looked through it; she could see the four men talking, but she couldn't hear them well. After a while, when she looked out again, the men had left and it was very quiet. There were no windows or ventilation in this impoverished bathroom. The whole room reeked of urine and human feces. The air that Fatima was breathing now was so heavy with acidic fumes that it was making her breathless and nauseous

It was pretty late. Sheraz was still at the hospital, and he had called me to inquire why Fatima hadn't returned yet. I was very fearful of where Fatima had gone.

The girls were very tired by now, and Sana fell asleep on my lap. I don't remember when I dozed off. It was the warmth on my wrist that woke me up. I felt I had slept only a few minutes, and the sun was already burning my skin. The bright patch on my wrist became hotter and hotter, and Sana woke up screaming, "Mom, it is so hot!" Suddenly I realized it wasn't the sun; it was still night. I peeped out of my window, and that's when I saw the fumes, and flames.

The shelter was on fire. I caught Sana in my arms; I ran to all the rooms and woke every one up. The smoke had begun to lace our breath. Somebody had locked our door from outside. We were trapped. Gopi took a blanket and broke the window glass. One by one we jumped out into the back yard.

The pigeons were frantic. Sana cried, "Mom, save the pigeons!" but there was not enough time and the gate had been locked, too. We had to climb over the high concrete wall. Our sweaty hands made it difficult to climb the wall and everyone kept slipping down. Then we decided to hoist each other up. I was the last to jump. The streets looked abandoned. It was strange why no one had noticed the fire and called for help.

Fatima had been in her prison far too long; it had been only an hour, but it seemed like a lifetime. She had to get out. Fatima began to push the door and kick it.

The door was pretty old and worn out. Her last dash at the door shattered it wide enough to get out.

The cool fresh air revived her senses again, and she wanted to go into the store and look for her gun. She wasn't sure if the men had returned, quietly she crept in like a spider. She peered over the counter, and she noticed that the gun was lying on an old black table. Slowly she stood up. All looked quiet and desolate, and Fatima dashed for the gun.

In her hurry, she bumped the table and the gun fell to floor. That's when she heard voices. She knew the men had returned. Fatima hid behind a huge bag of rice.

Her sweaty hand pulled the rice bag closer; she was very afraid. The men were in the same room as her, and she could hear them loud and clear. The four men were very elated. They were drinking and congratulating each other. Fatima's eyes were fixed on the gun and her mind was spinning ways of getting to it. It was Mohan's voice that shook her stare. What Mohan had just said, washed Fatima in a very cold sweat. Without any fear she stood up, disclosing herself.

Fatima ran towards Raju and slapped him. She pulled on his shirt and yelled, "What have you done now?"

Mohan and the others laughed at her, and said,

"Your yelling and screaming is of no use now. You can go if you want, since nobody can harm us now."

Fatima was very apprehensive of their newfound confidence. Mohan caught her hand firmly and said, "You see, we have left no evidence. We set fire to your shelter an hour ago – everyone must be dead by now, there is no one to support you or your dear Savita, who I'm sure is also dead by now."

Raju moved in very close to her, and grabbed her by her chin; he sniggered and said, "I don't think anyone will go to save them. All the neighbors' doors have been locked from the outside." They all laughed heinously. Fatima couldn't believe that human beings were capable of such diabolic acts.

With complete awareness and surety, Fatima walked straight to that black table, and picked up the gun. The cold metal strengthened her burning hands, and she let her finger slip onto the trigger. Her first shot killed Mohan, and next she chose to eliminate Raju.

Salman and Ravi jumped over the store counter and sprinted for the open street. Fatima threw the gun as far she could, and ran towards the shelter. There she saw the girls and me standing helplessly, watching the fire burn down all hope.

I was so confused and scared, but by now I had

gathered that this had been done intentionally to kill us. Fatima appeared from the thick smoke; it was a relief to see her. She at once took control.

Fatima said that we should go to my apartment, since no one knew that address around here. It was the most treacherous night; we walked on and on, barefoot and scared. At every street corner our hearts thumped harder. Mrs. Dave and Sheraz were at the hospital, we would have to inform them. Luckily my apartment was only two miles away. It was 5.30 am, and a milk dairy was just opening its shutters.

Fatima asked the dairy owner if we could make a phone call, and she told Sheraz what happened. We all dragged our feet up six floors, and fell flop at my flat door. All of us were very hungry and exhausted, but I guess we were so tired that no one requested food. We just fell asleep, wherever we found a spot. It was morning before we actually dozed off. I let everyone sleep in late. Fatima woke up quite early and was trying to call Sheraz to ask him about Savita's condition. Sheraz told her that they were planning to keep her in the hospital for at least a week, as she needed a lot of healing to regain her strength. I could hear Fatima talking to Sheraz in a very hushed voice. He also told her that Mrs. Dave had gone back to her hotel this morning, and would return by noon. Once Mrs. Dave got back to the hospital, then Sheraz would get out and come to the apartment. Fatima assured him that everyone was fine, and that's all that matters, things could always be built again.

I woke up around 11 am. Fatima was in the shower, and I started to make some arrangements for breakfast. I called the grocer, whose store was on the ground floor of our building, and ordered some basics, like eggs, milk, bread, and biscuits.

By the time Fatima was out from her shower, I had already started to chop onions, cilantro, and peppers for omelets. Fatima came into the kitchen with her wet long hair; she looked so serene and composed.

It looked as if nothing had happened, or that she had just washed away that horrid night. The aroma of the fresh, spicy omelets woke up all the girls. We spread a bed sheet on the floor and we sat down to eat. It felt weird. When only Ahmed, Sana, and I were in this flat, I would always complain that it was too cramped up.

Now there were nineteen of us, and no one felt the lack of space; instead it made us feel closer.

Ahmed called from Delhi. He had left two nights ago for a conference. Ahmed was totally unaware of what had happened here in the last few hours. He was flabbergasted when I gave him all the details. He decided to catch the next flight back.

I didn't stop him. I needed him, and I thought Sheraz would be more relaxed with Ahmed here. Ahmed was good at taking care of all legalities as he was a very practical and objective man; none of us were good at that.

We didn't know what to do next. Sheraz had filed a complaint with the police about the fire, but no one came to inquire at the shelter site. Fatima wasn't very hopeful about the police; she knew that they, too, had been paid off. Sheraz came to the apartment around 2.30 pm. He had picked up some kabobs and naan for our lunch. He looked very scared and restless. Fatima and I were warming the food up when Sheraz came out from his bath. He walked into the kitchen, and told us that today when he passed the shelter, a neighbor informed him that last night someone had shot Mohan and Raju. I was in shock. I just couldn't believe what was happening to this quiet, fun-loving town. It was suddenly falling into the grips of crime. Fatima didn't flinch at all but kept pouring out the tea, and Sheraz stared at her nervously. She put all the cups on a serving tray, and handed it to Sheraz without a word. Sheraz had lunch with us and then left for the hospital. Fatima went downstairs to see him off. I could see them from my balcony; they were holding hands and talking very seriously. I couldn't hear them from that distance. Finally Fatima, like a mother, placed her hands on his shoulders and smiled at him. Sheraz looked relieved, and he walked away with ease.

When Fatima came back upstairs, she looked very apprehensive. I sat her down with our favorite cup of chai, and asked her what was weighing on her mind.

She looked at me for a moment and then very hesitantly said, "Do you think after all that has happened to Savita, Mrs. Dave will still want to adopt her?" I wasn't honest with her, but this was exactly what was preying on my mind too.

I told Fatima that we should first pray that Savita recovers and heals fully. Sometimes the scars left on the body may heal, but those that were left on your soul rarely heal.

Fatima held my hand, gave me one of her healing smiles, and said, "She will heal; we just have to shower her with love, strength, and courage." That's when Fatima and I had our first and perhaps our last, heart-churning talk.

We had lost all our belongings in the shelter fire. Sheraz and Mrs. Dave had bought the girls some basic clothing and necessities. Fatima was wearing one of the new dresses that Sheraz had brought her. I think it had been a while since the girls had something new to wear. She looked at herself with a smile; she knew this new dress that Sheraz had bought her was filled with his love. She carried the pleasantness of the sky in this blue attire. The dress had pants and a scarf with it, and was embroidered with delicate silver paisleys.

Fatima came and sat down beside me in our balcony. We each had our hot cup of chai in our palms. We sipped them slowly, hoping it would unwind our tormented hearts. For some time Fatima remained quiet, and we just stared into our silent space. She kept gazing at the deep blue summer sky. It was just starting to get warm, and I could see a line of delicate little drops of perspiration form just around the curve of her upper lip.

Today I had actually observed Fatima; she was quiet pretty, and the pain that she held in her heart, gave her face a soft delicateness and glow.

I kept sipping my chai and thinking, if Fatima hadn't been born here, if she didn't have the destiny that she had now, how would she be?

My mother always told me, "Pain makes us more humane, it teaches us lessons of courage and faith." Fatima did have a lot of wisdom, and courage.

I was nearly done with my tea when Fatima suddenly looked at me very fondly.

She held my hand against her dry cheeks and said, "You remind me so much of your mother and you are becoming like her, too. You know these girls have a lot of hope in you." I smiled and said, "But I'm not God, what hope can I give them." She smiled again as if teasing me, "we have hope in human beings, and faith in God, don't worry you are cable of giving hope to many, I can see it in you."

"I need to share some truths with you. Maybe we will not be together again, and the truth about my life may never be known."

"Do you know I am not an orphan?" I looked at her with confused eyes, as I didn't know whether that was a good thing for her or not. Fatima took a deep sigh and began to reveal to me the secrets of her heart.

I was about nine years old and lived on the outskirts of this big city with my parents. We were very poor, my mother and father both worked as construction helpers. They were paid the bare minimum. I had a brother whose name was Iqbal, a year older than me. Often we had to sleep with empty stomachs, or just ate boiled rice. Every morning my parents and my brother would go to the construction sites to find work. I was left at home, since they didn't have work for young girls, so I stayed at home and did the chores. We had no running water or electricity. Sometimes I would walk two to three miles to fetch water from a water truck.

I had a friend then, who was a year younger than me, and her name was Seema. We loved each other. Our walks to fetch the water were the best part of our day.

We chatted all the way. The water truck guy charged us twenty-five paisa for a gallon. He was a nice guy named Harnam Singh. We called him Hari kaka.

He loved us kids, and sometimes he would bring us candy. Hari had an assistant with him who helped us fill the water, he was called Vasu. Vasu was about sixteen, and Seema and I didn't like him a bit. There was something about him that scared us because he would stare at us as if he would drink us up.

One day while I was waiting for Seema to get her water filled, I started chatting with Hari kaka. It was getting late and Seema was on the other side of the truck with Vasu. I got up and walked around to find her. Seema was nowhere to be seen. Suddenly I heard a meek cry from the bushes in the front. I ran there, I saw Vasu was trying to fondle Seema, and she was trying to push him away. My feet froze to the ground. I didn't know what to do, but I moved in and made myself visible. Seema was crying for help. I impulsively picked up a stone, and threw it at Vasu.

It startled him, and he let Seema go. I grabbed her hand, and we ran. On our way back home, we didn't talk, we were so eager to just get home, and in our rush we had left our water cans there. I knew Mom would be very angry, since we wouldn't have drinking water. But I was just happy that I had saved my friend. It was a very heavenly feeling. I felt as if I was special, and that this was my destiny, to save people.

Fatima continued with her story.

When we reached home, Seema was worried about how we would get water now, since Vasu would always be there. I told her we would think of something tomorrow. I was too exhausted to even think. When I entered my house, the scene there was worse. My father had had a bad fall from one of the building sites and broke his leg. They had to amputate it. I was horrified; my mother sat there crying helplessly in one corner. My brother was consoling my father that he would get better, and all would be fine. I was flabbergasted, I didn't know what was I supposed to do. I just fell flop on the ground at my mother's feet, and sobbed away.

Fatima inhaled deeply, then started speaking again.

Days passed by and now Mother was going to work with my brother, while I was taking care of Father. Luckily, Seema's brother offered to get our water for us. I was happy; Seema would be safe with him. Mother couldn't bring enough money home and half of the money was going to Father's medicine. That night we all slept on an absolutely empty stomach. Mom told me to just drink a lot of water and you won't feel hungry. But my stomach kept groaning. The whole night, I could hear Mother and Father talking in a very low tone, so that we wouldn't get disturbed. I could hear that Mom was crying, and at one point I heard Father sob too. What I never realized was that they were deciding the course of my life.

Next morning, Father told me that we all had to go to the city, to see about some job for him there. We were moving. I panicked – how could I leave Seema behind? I asked Mom if we could take her, after all she lived alone with her brother who was always quite mean to her. Mother asked me to quickly go and say goodbye to Seema. How could I? It would kill her, and it was already killing me. Mother finished the packing in a few minutes; we didn't have anything, just the clothes on our backs, and a few pots. Seema was sitting outside her house, washing her pots and pans. She thought I was there to play with her. I didn't know how to break her heart, so I just hugged her, kissed her all over, and told her, 'I'll never forget you,' and I ran away.

We took two small trains to get to the city. As soon as we got off at Purjang Station, we felt overwhelmed by the crowd. This was a small town in Lucknow, but coming from a very small, remote village, it gave us city fear. I was clutching Mom's hands, Father held on to Iqbal. I was tired and hungry. Right near the station was this big house. I could see a lot of kids playing in the front yard.

Father looked at my mother in a very strange way, and she suddenly looked very nervous. She sat me down under a banyan tree and said, 'It's nice and shady here. You sit here, Father and me have to go ahead to see about that job, we will fetch you from here on our way back.' I readily agreed. I was very tired and I was enjoying seeing those kids play.

When they started to leave, my mother came and gave me a strong hug, she wiped the sweat off my forehead and said, 'Don't be afraid. You are my brave little girl, and I love you.' Then she caught my brother's hands, and followed my father, who had already moved way ahead. I yelled out, 'Goodbye, father.' I guess he didn't hear me, he didn't look back at me.

Tears were running out of my eyes, but Fatima continued with her herculean courage.

Six hours later, it was 8:30 pm, and very dark, and I was still sitting under that tree. I don't know when I dozed off, but when I awoke it was morning, and I was still waiting for my parents. Now the kids in the big house were doing some chores. I opened the gate and walked in. Just then a big, huge man came toward me yelling. He kept trying to tell me that I couldn't come in. He looked like a policeman. Later he told me that he was the gatekeeper for this orphanage.

I explained my plight to him, and he took me in. The inside of this big house didn't look so impressive. It had a certain gloom and mustiness to it. All of the walls needed paint, and the floors needed new tiles. The best thing that I liked was that there were lots of kids in there. Till then I didn't know what an orphanage was, and who were these kids? Then the gatekeeper took me to the manager of the house.

His name was Jagan Singh. He told me that my parents had abandoned me, and they were never coming back for me. I refused to believe him, but I asked him if I could stay here till they came back for me. He said it wasn't possible, since I had parents and wasn't an orphan. I was terrified, and he knew that I had no one, and nowhere to go. Jagan acted very sympathetic to me, and said that this would be our little secret; he would let me stay there as an orphan, and wouldn't tell the owners the truth. I would get to eat, and get a mat to sleep on, just like all the kids, and I would do the chores that were allotted to me. I was so thankful to him. He took me in and introduced me to the rest of the gang. Jagan again reminded me that I shouldn't tell anyone that I had parents, and that he would tell the gatekeeper that if anyone came looking for me he should let him know. That was settled, and a new chapter of my life began. The first few months there were quite nice. I was starting to lose hope of ever seeing my parents, but I was comfortable. What bothered me was why Mother had not left Iqbal with me, and why did they want to abandon me? I had not done anything wrong. As I got friendly with the girls there, I realized that there were a few others who had been left at this gate just like me. One of the older girls told that it could be because we were girls, and that it was easy to abandon us – since sons can work and take care of the parents, we girls are just burdens on poor parents.

I was in shock and could not stop my tears from escaping my eyes. One of the girls informed me that she had been abandoned by her mother and brother twelve years ago, and she still hoped that one day they would come back for her.

I interrupted Fatima, and asked how she could live with all this. Fatima continued:

It was our fear and insecurity that had bonded us

together. We were scared to let go of what little we had, for that was all we had. It had been six months now, and what the girls had been telling me was finally making its way into my heart: I was not wanted. Every little bit of free time we had, we would sit in the yard and talk about whatever we remembered from our past, but time was slowly blurring those memories. I missed Seema and talked about her a lot. I wondered whether her life was better than mine. We all slept in one huge room; there were forty-seven girls, and the boys, who were sixteen in number, slept in a different room. I don't think time will ever blur this memory of mine, when for the first time Jagan Singh touched me.

Late that night, the door to our sleeping room cracked open. I could see a shadow standing between the light and the darkness. This shadow came inside the room. Someone was walking towards me. I thought I was dreaming, I rubbed my eyes. The moonlight from the window gave a face to this shadow, it was Jagan. I got up, as I thought he needed some tea or something. Jagan had never come to our room at night, at least not in the time I was here. He sat down next to me on the floor and before I could ask him anything, he placed his hands on my mouth, and pushed me back to lie down. Then he came very close to me and whispered in my ears, 'This is our second secret that you can't tell anyone.' And he began to molest me.

The girl who was sleeping next to me, was older than me; she could definitely see what he was doing to me. We were forty-seven in that room and no one stopped him. The next morning I went into the toilet and I cried with pain, shame, and loss.

For the first time, I was angry at my mother, and that day I made a promise to myself that I would never forgive her. In the daytime, Jagan would treat me normally, as if nothing had happened, but at night, every night, he would become a different man, a vicious monster. There were so many people around me, and I could tell anyone; but I did not need to, for they all knew. Every month an elderly man used to come to the office, he would be very well dressed, and came in a fancy car. Jagan Singh would dote over him, and later this man would come and give us very nice food to eat. The gatekeeper told me that this rich man was the owner of the center and financed everything we had or needed. As he was leaving, one little girl ran to him, and told him that the floor hurts her and asked if he could bring her a bed next time. He was overwhelmed by her innocence, and right away he told Jagan that he wanted to inspect the sleeping quarters, which normally he never did. Seeing the shambles that we were sleeping in, he was very furious, and had a long and stern argument with Jagan. The very next day forty-seven wooden beds were delivered to our home. The beds had made every one of us very happy except Jagan. The bed was wide enough only for one person, but that did not deter Jagan. He would pull me down onto the floor, under the bed, and continue his torture. Every night I prayed that someone would come and save me. Sometimes I felt I was letting this torture happen to me, all because I was a girl, useless and unwanted even by my mom who was a woman like me. Maybe this was my destiny, a huge tax, to have a roof on my head and some morsels of food to live on

One day when I was helping out in the kitchen, that older girl came to me and told me, 'Don't be such a martyr. You are not his only victim, as we all have gone through this.' I was shocked, and she continued, 'And why do you think he lets us stay here? He likes young girls. Once you are thirteen, he will stop and look for another younger girl.'

I couldn't believe the words I was listening to. I knew now why they had not come to my rescue – how could they save me, when they couldn't save themselves? This didn't make me feel better, although the other girl had intended to pacify me; it made me feel very horrid and dirty. A year later I got my first period, and he stopped raping me. I was told that now I could get pregnant, and he wouldn't want that hanging on his throat, as he would get caught. We were all over thirteen by now, and for the next two months we all slept in peace. Then, on a Wednesday afternoon, the gatekeeper found another girl at our gate. She was only six years old, and her name was Seema. I felt as if my lost friend had come back to me, and I loved her from the very moment she told me her name.

Seema was really an orphan. Her parents had drowned in a flood, and her relatives refused to take her in, so they left her here. She had a note with her that explained all of this. Seema was soaking with sweat, her little dirty dress looked more like a rag. She had lovely eyes, intense and mysterious, just like the colors of the sky at dusk. Jagan touched her cheeks devilishly, and smiled impishly at me. I took Seema by her hand, and told him, that I would show her around and get her settled. Then he spilled out his venom, which would slowly kill her. He told Seema that we don't house such young girls here, but if she behaves and does all that he tells her, he will let her live here. Seema had tears in her eyes, she was terrified. She looked at me, and said, 'But I have nowhere else to go.'

Jagan came close to her, and knelt beside her. He wiped off her tears and said, 'That's ok, you just remember about this favor of mine.' I wanted to kill him – what a snake he was. Now I understood that this was the line that hung like a sword on our necks.

As I was walking swiftly away with Seema, Jagan called out and said, 'Now, isn't she a sweet thing.' I didn't realize that in my anger I was squeezing Seema's hand too tightly. She complained, and I pulled her to a corner and asked her, 'Why did you have to come here? You should have gone to some other home.' Seema didn't understand what

I was muttering away. She called me 'didi' which means elder sister, and said, 'I am very thirsty, and hungry, can I please have something to eat?'

I watched Seema very closely and saw to it that she was never alone with Jagan. Every night I would make her sleep next to my bed. She loved the attention, but was totally unaware of my fears.

Here Fatima stopped for a second and had a sip of her now cold chai, then continued with her story.

Two months had passed, and I and the other girls felt relaxed. Perhaps Seema was too young for him, and he was not interested. My anger and hatred for Jagan was giving the other girls not only a vent, but was raising their own fury. All these pent up feeling were churning in us, and we began for the first time to cherish ourselves. We had promised each other that we wouldn't let anyone harm us again.

One afternoon, as per my usual schedule, I went for a bath. Seema was playing inside with some girls. I was out from my bath within twenty minutes. I went into my room and started to comb my hair. I was feeling that something was not right, it was too quiet. One of the girls who was playing with Seema came to me and said, 'When will

Seema come back? It's her turn to throw the dice.' I told her to go and look for her. She then went on to tell me that, as soon as I went for my bath, Jagan came in and took her to the kitchen. She said he told her that, he had some special candy only for her.

The comb fell from my hands, as if I had lost all sensation. I ran like a crazy person straight to the kitchen. To my utmost horror, no one was there. I ran through all the rooms, and came back to the kitchen again. My frenzied behavior put all the girls on alert and they were all following my search. I kept asking Seema's friend, 'Are you sure he took her to the kitchen?' and she replied yes, then she said something very innocently that raised all the hair on my body: 'Maybe he took her to the pantry, that's where he had taken me, too, to give me candy.'

Meena, the eldest girl and I both stared at the closed pantry door. Meena held my hand very hopefully and said, 'I know where he hides his extra set of keys.' She ran and came back with the keys. I grabbed the keys from her, and banged open the door. The storeroom air was filled with tiny fibers of wheat husk, and a strong smell of spices. We couldn't see anyone; it was too dark, as someone had removed the light bulb. Just as we were about to give up our hunt, I heard a meek cry of pain. That voice took me back to my childhood, as if everything was happening again.

I kept moving inside the pantry, trying very hard to see where I was going by the dim light that filtered through the dusty ventilation. I stepped on something cold on the floor. It felt like a kitchen knife. I held onto the knife as I dared to push on ahead. Suddenly, from behind the gunny bags of grains, Jagan Singh appeared.

He was all sweaty, and furious. He ordered me to, get out.

That's when I saw Seema squatting on the floor besides his feet. She was crying, but she saw me, and gathered the courage to stand up. Then she said, 'It's too dark here, I'm scared, and I don't want your candy.' Seema ran past me, and went to Meena. Jagan glared at me and tried to walk past me. As soon as his breath touched my skin, I lost control. I wanted to beat him up, and I thought that's what I was doing. What I forgot was that I was holding a knife in my hand – I was not hitting him, I was stabbing him. I kept stabbing him till he collapsed and fell over me. The sound of the girls yelling in fear woke me from my spell of hate. I pushed Jagan's body off me, and came out into the lighted kitchen area. All the girls were there, they all had once again witnessed a grave crime. I stared into their fearful faces and went to my room. As usual, no one spoke. I knew they had already been rendered dumb by Jagan and were now not only dumb, but also deaf and blind with fear.

I changed my bloody clothes; I hugged Seema very dearly and told her that she had nothing to fear. I walked outside the orphanage; the gatekeeper, as usual, was dozing. I closed the gate behind me, looked at all the girls watching me leave, and I never turned back again. I kept walking aimlessly for miles, I didn't know where I was going, but destiny knew.

I stopped outside your mother's home, and she took me in. The police never came looking for me. As I had assumed correctly, none of the girls would tell that I killed Jagan.

I gathered my courage to interrupt her story, and I told Fatima, "I knew that you had killed the manager, from my mother's book." Then I assured her that even though the book had been sent for publishing, I had changed all the names and locations, and that no one would guess it was her.

Fatima smiled at me, and told me, "I'm not worried. Destiny is playing a very funny game with me, and I'm just waiting for the next turn, whatever it maybe.

I need to tell you something that no one knows till now. I am telling you this, not because I am proud of it, but because it had to be done, and once again destiny chose me."

"You know that night when Savita was raped, she had whispered to me the names of the men who had raped her."

I looked at Fatima, horrified. "Men?"

"Yes!" Fatima said. "She was gang raped by four men." I couldn't believe what Fatima had just uttered. I was trembling with disgust and hatred for the atrocities that had been committed on that poor girl; I had never seen or known such inhuman behavior. I trembled with the thought of how this little child might have suffered such horrible, horrible pain.

Fatima told me that it was the grocer and his friends. I remembered that Fatima had not gone with Sheraz to the hospital when Sheraz took Savita. I had seen Fatima go into the shelter storeroom, and now she told me the reason. She had gone to take Sheraz's revolver.

I was too scared to listen, but Fatima slowly and in every gory detail disclosed to me the events of that night.

I wasn't shocked, I was actually shaken, Fatima, who was sitting so calmly in front of me, had killed two human beings a few days ago.

I was terrified, but Fatima had such confidence. I knew then that every fiber in her being believed that she had done the right thing.

She looked away from me, and once again stared at the vast sky. "The two men who escaped are in hiding, but I'm sure they will come out and inform the police about me."

"I know you might think that I have sinned, as I had no right to take a life away, but why did destiny put me in this situation? Why couldn't I be like everyone else, and be quiet about it? I have no answer to the games that destiny has played with me. I know of so many people who have committed atrocities, yet they wander this earth free and unpunished."

Fatima spoke as if she was in a trance; she wasn't talking to me, but to her crying soul. She said, "If these hands today are covered with the blood of the men who destroyed my Savita's life, that is because it was these very hands that hugged her and wiped her tears."

Her whole appearance changed. Fatima suddenly looked so drained and exhausted, as if a massive burden had been vented, and even her sky blue dress looked pale and dead grey now. She saw that I was overwhelmed by everything, and she had a true understanding of my endurance level. Fatima clasped both my hands in hers and said, "It's all done, don't worry, leave everything to God. When I have no fear, why do you let fear rule you?"

At that moment I realized that destiny had also engraved my role in this world.

It may not be like that of Fatima, but I have to play my role. There were people like Mohan, who were sinners, then there were people like Savita, who would be wronged, and then Fatima's role was to punish these sinners, and my role would be from now on to tell these untold stories. I realized that there are no accidents in life; Fatima was right, things happen in our lives because they were meant to happen.

Fatima told me that Sheraz had called from the hospital, and that they would be discharging Savita tomorrow. She also told me that Sheraz wanted me and Fatima to go to the contractor, and give him instructions to start the rebuilding of the shelter.

Mrs. Dave had called her friends abroad, and they all had sent funds.

I was very happy to see that while evil could destroy, goodness could rebuild.

At around 11am the next morning, Savita came back from the hospital. Fatima had warned all the girls that they should act very casual with her. We had to try to make Savita forget the event. Fatima put it very plainly to the girls: "She was hurt badly, now she has healed, and she needs to move on. Remember that any event in life should not stop you from living."

Mrs. Dave and Fatima took Savita to her bed. She liked the new arrangement, and was happy that all the girls were sleeping in one room. The closeness created by the lack of space gave her a feeling of security. Savita asked when they would return to the shelter, and why were they living here in my flat. Fatima convinced her that due to an electrical malfunction, there had been a big fire in the shelter.

She asked about her pigeons, and I told her that Sana had set them free, so they were fine. All the girls tried to keep her happy; they played her favorite games with her. Sheraz and Fatima sat quietly at my breakfast table, sipping chai. Our doubts had been laid to rest when Sheraz told us that Mrs. Dave had booked her and Savita's tickets for next week. Fatima didn't seem too happy, but Sheraz kept convincing her that the sooner Savita got out from these surroundings, the easier it would be for her to start a fresh life. What Sheraz did not understand was that Fatima had become very attached to Savita. Sheraz wasn't even aware of the extent of Fatima's love for Savita. I placed my hand on Fatima's shoulder and said, "It's all for the betterment of her life, you have to let her go." Fatima realized it was time to set this pigeon free. That day Sheraz, Savita, and Mrs. Dave slept for sixteen hours; we didn't wake them up, as they needed that rest.

I kept wondering if Fatima had told Sheraz about Mohan. I didn't feel I could tell Ahmed about Fatima's story; it was something that I wanted to keep to myself, till the right time appeared to speak it out.

I had this innate feeling that Fatima knew that Sheraz would not be able to handle the truth, and so she did not burden him. She always treated him with deep compassion, as if he was the one who needed to be saved. Every time I would see Sheraz and

Fatima speak to each other, there was this restlessness, a discomfort; about an untold truth. But they knew each other so well that things could be left unspoken between them. They trusted each other, and Sheraz knew or had accepted that Fatima would do whatever she felt was right.

Even though Fatima did not agree with Sheraz's way of dealing with anger and fear, she never contradicted him. She knew that each one of us have our own way of dealing with pain and loss. Fatima knew that it was because of this nature of his, of not putting down people or hating them, that Sheraz had accepted Fatima so willingly. This was his unique way of healing or letting go. Sheraz was a very humble person. He would always say that he was in no position to judge or punish anyone, but that he could only help them to heal.

29

The work of reconstructing the shelter had started. Now that Savita was back from the hospital, Sheraz was fully engaged with the rebuilding.

We had lost everything in the shelter fire – all our belongings, whether material stuff or memories, they were all charred to dust. Everything else was replaceable, but what was really hurting me, was seeing Mom's memories destroyed. Sheraz knew about this, and so one morning before leaving for the shelter, he whispered to me, "Come down to the shelter with me, I want to show you something." The work was going on in full swing, and I realized as I walked through the unfinished rooms that Sheraz had kept the same floor plan as the original house. I was very touched and surprised that he had remembered such details. Then he took me to one of the finished rooms. When he opened the door, the room was fully furnished, and every piece of furniture had been replaced with an exact replica of the original one. Mom's dresser stood gallantly on the left corner of the room, where it used to be when Mom was alive.

I couldn't control my tears, and they rolled down my smiling cheeks. Sheraz had taught me a very valuable lesson that time may take away everything from us, but it can never take away our love. With love we can recreate everything again, well, at least the valuable things.

What was most important to all of us was that Mom's mission to preserve life, had to go on. People live and die, but goodness should always stay alive.

Savita and Mrs. Dave's flight was for Wednesday, so we had just four more days with Savita. Fatima had gone shopping and bought some new clothes for her and a little clay toy pigeon. Savita was very happy with the toy, but she was terrified of leaving Fatima. Fatima had been the mother that Savita had always wanted. I was watching Fatima pack Savita's suitcase, and I could also see those tears that she was hiding. Savita just couldn't understand why she had to go. Fatima convinced her that her life would be better with Mrs. Dave, and that she couldn't get that kind of future here with Fatima and Sheraz. Fatima wanted to keep her here, but she knew that there were too many dangers here.

That last night, Fatima did not sleep; I saw her go into Savita's room at around 2 am. To her surprise, Savita was still awake.

Fatima brought her into the kitchen for a warm glass of milk. As Savita sat there drinking the milk, I walked in, too, and sat beside her. Savita looked at both of us and with a trembling voice said, "I am scared, I don't think I can go." Fatima couldn't resist the plea in her voice, and she picked her up in her arms. We walked out to the balcony. The stars shone so brightly, Fatima gazed into them, and then, with their twinkle in her eyes, she looked at Savita. Fatima noticed a scar on Savita's chest; it was from the ordeal that she had gone through. Suddenly Fatima's eyes twinkled more; she touched the scar on Savita and said, "Do you know how you got this scar?" Savita didn't have much recollection of the horrific event. Fatima took advantage of this and said, "Remember, you were at the hospital because you were hurt, that's when the doctors saw that your heart had been hurt badly." Savita started to look at her scar, it ran right across her chest, Fatima continued, "The doctors wanted to give you a new heart, but they couldn't find one your size."

She tickled Savita and said, "Because you are such a peanut."

Savita giggled, and asked, "Then what did the doctors do?"

Fatima told her, "All they could find was a heart of a baby lion, so they had to put that in you; after all you needed a new heart."

Savita's face flashed with amazement. "You mean to say I have the heart of a lion in me now?" She asked Fatima apprehensively, "Will I be able to live with this heart?"

Fatima kissed her and said, "You will not only be able to live, but you will live as bravely as a lion, nothing will scare you."

Savita looked at me with gleaming eyes, then she looked at Fatima, and kissed her back, and said, "No wonder I feel so strong." We all laughed and hugged each other, and at that moment, beyond those dark clouds, the sun began to rise.

That day Savita was all thrilled and excited about her trip. She kept telling us that we all had to come and visit her, and we all assured her that we would. Fatima was quiet; Savita asked her if she was coming to the airport to drop her off. Fatima told her she had to stay here and take care of things, but Sheraz and Ahmed would go with them.

All the stuff was packed in the taxi. Mrs. Dave said her farewell to all the girls, and also handed them some cash gifts. It was time for Fatima to let go of her dear Savita.

Fatima knelt down beside her, held her tiny hands, and said, "Don't forget me, remember this life is a gift to you from God, and you deserve to live it happily.

You are brave, you are strong, and most of all you are very precious." Savita let her tears roll.

She lovingly put her arms around Fatima's shoulders and said, "I know I am your lion-heart girl."

Fatima fondly held that tiny hand for the last time and said, "Go live your life." Somehow I knew that even though Savita was at a very immature age, she would never forget Fatima.

30

My daughter Sana was very upset that her dear friend Savita had to leave.

Fatima and I spent many hours trying to console her. Fatima's son was also very upset, as these two kids felt as if Savita had abandoned them. The whole day, no one spoke to each other much. We all were still digesting the fact that Savita had gone so far away from us. It felt like the longest day of our lives, everything was so lifeless and still.

I knew that Fatima was very worried. I knew she wanted to go to the airport, but she knew that if she did, Savita might have not left without her. I was very restless, I wanted to feel that there was still life, and said to Fatima, "Let's go to the shelter, and check out the construction work." Fatima agreed right away, as if she too needed to get out and divert her mind. I knew she was already going insane with anxiety over what was happening there at the airport. Sheraz and Ahmed would be back from the airport by 9 pm; it would take them a whole day in the journey back and forth, and of course they would wait there till the flight left.

Fatima boiled some eggs for the girls for dinner, and decided that we would do the groceries on our way back from the shelter. We both walked the streets like zombies; both our minds were far away. Fatima's mind was with Savita and my mind was with Fatima.

I dreaded to think of what she had done, and what the consequences would be; it was too much reality for me to handle.

I noticed that Fatima was in no rush to reach the shelter. It was a two-mile walk, and I suggested taking a rickshaw, but she said the walk will help her calm her mind. At one point on the road, she stopped and looked back, as if she was waiting for someone. I asked her about this, and she just smiled and said, "It's weird, but I felt as if someone was following me." I knew she was thinking of Savita, who always tagged along with her everywhere.

I don't know why, but these words just slipped from my mouth: "Wouldn't you like to find out where your parents are?"

She looked as if she already knew that this thought had invaded my mind, and without any emotion she said, "Why? For them I died many years ago, that's why they never came looking for me." She then said, "Sheraz and our son, and these girls are all the family I need."

We had just reached the entrance of the shelter. They were putting up the name board, and there in the center of the compound stood a marble statue of a mother holding her child in her arms. This was a new addition, as per Sheraz's new design. Fatima approached the statue and very gently touched the face of the child and said, "May she have a blessed life." Then she stood in front of the statue and squinted her eyes, to avoid the sun's glare. She looked very knowingly, then turned to me and said, "I think the face of this woman looks a lot like your mother."

I stared at the face, and I was amazed to see that she was right. She said that the sculptor had never seen my mother, yet how then did it resemble her? I walked towards the right side of the statue, and as I saw the statue from this angle, the profile looked a lot like Fatima, and I told her so. Fatima walked to the left side and said, "If you notice from this side the face resembles you."

I smiled and said, "Well if it looks like my mother, then from some angle it will look like me."

We both smiled at each other, Fatima then laid another piece of her wisdom on me by saying, "We see what we want to see. This shelter wouldn't be complete without a mother. After your mother passed away, I was pushed into that role, and now you are already filling these shoes so well." I didn't agree, I told her I was too weak and insecure to take on that role.

She smiled at me and said, "Life has already chosen you, you don't have a choice. I think none of us have a choice – we do what life intends us to do, to fulfill our purpose in this world."

Then Fatima said something that kind of scared me. She held my hand and said, "Promise me that if something happens to me, you will take care of my son and Sheraz."

I didn't know what to say, and so I said, "I can't take that responsibility, and where are you going, anyway?" She again gave me one of her very mysterious smiles that always suggested that she knows more than she's saying.

She said, "I worry for Sheraz, he is a very frail

person, too humble and honest for this world, but maybe, my absence might make him strong." I was looking scared and worried, but she laughed and consoled me, "Don't worry, everything will be fine, after all I can't do anything for anyone. It is God who is taking care of all of us, so let's just leave it to Him." We walked around the unfinished shelter. Fatima seemed very pleased, and I liked it too. It was much better than the older model, and now seemed stronger and more functional. There was more room, so more girls could be accommodated. The feeling around the shelter was not that positive, the neighbors were still very apprehensive about the authenticity of this shelter.

The grime that the grocer had spread about this place was still shading their thinking. It is very difficult for people to think well; the first thoughts that come into our minds are always negative, especially if it concerns females.

Fatima didn't care about the looks that we both were getting as we left the shelter. Some men started following and taunting us. Fatima held my hand tightly and said, "Just ignore them; they are doing only that which they are capable of."

The sun was really hot, even though it was only

6 pm. Fatima insisted on walking back. I rebelled; I was exhausted mentally and physically, there was this unexplained fear that was draining every nerve in me.

We started to look for a rickshaw, but at this time of the day, it was very difficult getting a ride. I think we had walked for nearly half a mile, with no sign of transportation. Fatima seemed very apprehensive; she still kept looking back over her shoulder, every few steps.

I think it was her fear which was affecting me. I kept getting a feeling of doom. As we waited at a street corner to rest, I tried to rationalize my anxiety. "I'm sure Savita is doing ok, and the flight might be on time."

Fatima looked at me very relieved, "Yes I think that's what's worrying me too."

Her flight was to leave at 7 pm, it was 7 pm now, and I think Savita might be thinking of us, that's why we both felt an ache in our hearts.

Just then we spotted a rickshaw and he was ready to take us to the market place. It felt nice, and the speeding rickshaw let the wind feel cooler.

I could see from a distance the smog and dust covering the busy area. As soon as we got off at the crammed market street, I had a pang of hunger rip my stomach. The whole place smelled of delicious kabobs and fresh bread. I asked Fatima if we could stop at one of these restaurants and eat something because we both needed some nourishment.

I ordered some nahari and naan, Fatima just ordered a cold glass of lassi. I was embarrassingly hungry; Fatima kept sipping her cold drink and smiled at my gluttony. It was a very small street restaurant, the people there were mostly men, Fatima noticed some men staring and laughing at me. She in return gave them a scorching stare; they got up and left quietly. I smiled at her and said, "You can be a good bodyguard."

She looked at me very lovingly and said, "You can take care of yourself, you just don't trust yourself." Fatima paid our bill and we started for the vegetable market. The hustle bustle of the market made us very relaxed and we strangely felt safe now. Fatima looked very relaxed as well.

Fatima said, "Since the girls have had a bad few days, why not make a special chicken dish for them? After all, it has been a while since they ate proper food."

I hated the smell that emits from fresh meat, so I never went into a butcher's shop. I told Fatima that I would just wait on the street for her, while she bought the chicken.

There was this nice utensil and kitchen store next to the butcher's shop, so I went in, and decided to buy some much-needed new pots and pans for the shelter. As always, I went overboard with my shopping; in the end there were five big boxes of stuff that I had just paid for. The storekeeper asked me for my address, and said that if I lived close by, he could deliver the stuff. That was a big relief to me, because Fatima and I would never be able to carry all this stuff. I came out from the store to show my apartment building to the shopkeeper. Our building was just a block away and was clearly visible from there. As I stood there pointing out to our tall blue building, I heard a commotion behind me.

The shopkeeper heard the noise, too. We looked behind, and I saw the culmination of my fears. There, about a few feet away from us, was a horde of policemen and two very angry boys, pointing at someone ahead of them. I recognized the boys at once; they were friends of the grocer whom Fatima had killed. These were the two boys who had escaped Fatima's wrath, and now they had come for revenge. It was only when they were about a hundred feet away from me that I realized that their fingers were pointing at me.

I was stunned. The situation had just hit me, and I knew I had to warn Fatima. It was very clear they were looking for her. I ran to the butcher's shop where Fatima was still finishing her order. I grabbed her hand. My look of fear spelt out everything I needed to say. She dropped my hand and ran towards the back door of the store. Within seconds she was gone, and the police were surrounding me. The inspector demanded to know where Fatima was, and said that she was wanted for murder. It all felt like a horrible nightmare. Everyone was sweating profusely, and the air felt suffocating. I was shivering with fear, I wasn't used to this type of reality, I couldn't speak. That's when the storekeeper informed them that he had seen a girl escape from his back door. Like the wind, the whole gang of officers disappeared.

The shopkeeper rudely asked me to leave; he handed me my money back and said, "We don't sell to murderers." I didn't care, I was worried about Fatima and was looking for her, standing there on the same spot where Fatima had left me in a paralyzed kind of state; my eyes fearfully scanned the street.

After about twenty minutes, I could hear the roar of angry voices again. This time the noise was mixed with yells of pain. It was Fatima's voice; I dared to look in the direction from where the noise seemed to be approaching. In the middle of the crowd of angry policemen, I saw Fatima smoldered in mud and sweat, being beaten like a slave.

I was shaken, but some strength in me made me run towards her. I tried to get in-between to save her. I yelled at the officers, and told them that they had no right to hit a women like this. I could see Fatima was bleeding from her forehead; someone from the angry mob had stoned her. Her clothes were ripped in many places. I grabbed a bed sheet from a nearby store and covered her.

The officer, wiping his sweat away, informed me that she was a criminal, and hence she deserved no mercy. I could see Fatima lying on the street, and every few seconds those so-called upholders of law and order kept kicking this helpless woman. The inspector explained to me that she had killed two men, and she had tried to escape from the law.

At that I retaliated and said, "Not men, savages who raped a nine-year-old girl."

The officer just smiled at me sarcastically and said,

"Madame, that's for the court to decide. My job was to capture the killer."

My mind couldn't connect these words with Fatima: "A killer, a criminal."

Two of the policemen grabbed both of Fatima's hands and dragged her to the outside street. They seated her on the pavement. The inspector asked for a jug of water, and splashed the water on Fatima's face.

Fatima was struggling even to breathe; she kept trying desperately to cover her body with the bed sheet. Blood mixed with saliva was dripping from the side of her mouth. My heart ached as it never had; I couldn't see her that way.

I pushed through the gaping, callous crowd and sat on the street near her feet.

I held her trembling hands, and pushed her hair away from her face. Fatima's eyes were as red as blood, they were not searing with tears, but with anger. She looked like a wounded tiger. She was breathing very strongly.

She collected a few breaths and spoke to me, "I'm all right, and this was going to happen, please take care of my family."

One of the constables hit her hard on her back

with his shaft, and asked her to get up. That was the last bit of her patience which the officer had stepped on.

Fatima stood up, snarling like a wild animal. She looked as if she was possessed, and she took the stick from the officer and began to hit him, till he was begging for mercy.

I had never seen Fatima this way; she swung the stick around, and let out a mind-shattering roar of anger. To my amazement, everyone moved away from her; they had sticks and guns, yet they stood there numbed in fear.

She stood shaking with intense emotion, and then she declared, "Nobody touches me. You want to arrest me, fine, I am coming with you, but if anyone lays a finger on me, I will kill him." There was complete silence; some people even dropped their weapons. The whole street was filled with people who were there to just watch a show; a new police van came onto the street.

A senior officer got out from the van, and very formally told Fatima, "Please don't create a scene, just step into the police van; we have your arrest warrant."

Fatima silently put down the stick, and an exhausted calm flushed her entire being as she started to walk towards the van.

The officer clasped one hand with a handcuff, and dragged her with the other. As she was obediently walking towards her destiny, the two boys who had brought the police here to arrest her pushed their way next to her.

They both giggled heinously and taunted her, "You were going to kill us – tough luck, now you are the one who will die."

I was only a few steps behind Fatima, She turned towards the two boys and smiled at them very sympathetically, which confused them.

Within a split second, Fatima grabbed the pistol from the inspector's holster, and slammed it against the boy's forehead. There was a struggle between Fatima and the inspector, who was trying to get his gun back. During that time, Fatima refused to let the pistol budge from that boy's forehead. Everyone noticed that the nervous boy peed in his pants. Fatima smiled now, in a very content way, and willingly gave the gun back to the cop.

She moved very close to that boy and said, "You are dead already." Before any of us could conceive the implication of her statement, Fatima turned towards the angry mob. In a very loud and declarative voice she announced, "I have killed two men. They had raped a nine-year-old girl, my daughter. These two men were a part of that rape, and I didn't get a chance to kill them." Then she looked at the cops and said, "and these two rapists will wander freely because they are sons of rich and politically connected fathers, so they will never be arrested. I leave them in your community; you decide whether your daughters would be safe around them."

Suddenly the mob of spectators realized that they were just being led like sheep. Fatima had awakened them and showed them their real target. The boys sensed the building wrath of the crowd and tried to slip away. One woman, who was at a very frail age, picked up her slipper and started to beat these boys vehemently.

Some unquenched need for justice had inspired her to seize the moment. Within few seconds, the anger spread like a fire and the boys were engulfed in this pent-up fury.

The police were distracted by the out-of-control mob. The officers started to try to cool them off, but it was like a riot, and no one could stop that awakening.

Everyone on the street had suffered some kind

of injustice or degradation in his or her life; they couldn't lose this opportunity to vent.

A gust of dust and fumes blew out from the center of this circle, it looked like a rising tornado. Fatima saw an opportunity – she grabbed my hand and pulled me outside the eye of that tornado.

She held my hand and kept walking towards the police van that was now abandoned and empty. All the cops were trying to prevent a riot from happening. Fatima sat on the footstep of the van; I obediently sat next to her. I looked around; there was no one around for about a few yards, and I thought it was a good chance for Fatima to escape. I got up and dragged Fatima up, and said, "Run away, there is no one here."

Fatima gave me one of her wisdom-filled smile, and sat down on the van step again. Seeing me so confused and flustered she said, "I am tired. I am tired of looking over my shoulder, and I am tired of fighting with my conscience."

I was still confused, and I pleaded with her, "Once you are sent to jail, they may sentence you to death. This is your only chance, you are capable of so much good, why do you want to end this life?"

Fatima pulled on my hand and drew me down

next to her. "I have done what I could do, what destiny had planned for me. I am not afraid of death, I deserve this punishment."

I shook her up and said, "You didn't do anything wrong, you have saved many helpless girls."

Fatima patted my shoulder lovingly and said, "Violence should never be the answer to any problem, no one has a right to either hurt or kill anyone. I am sorry that I couldn't find a better solution."

I still wasn't ready to listen to any explanation, because I knew that if instead of Savita it had been Sana, I would have done the same.

Fatima could read my thoughts and she said, "You are an educated woman, you don't have to do what I did. You can find a better and a legal solution."

Then Fatima said something that changed my mind forever: "You know, we blame everyone else for our problem, that's why the problem never goes away." I stared at her, very baffled, yet was eager to listen to her solution. "We women are to be blamed for the misery we suffer in this world. We love our daughters, our mothers, our sisters, but when it comes to their rights, we expect them to bend, and give way to the men."

I felt like a huge curtain was being lifted from my

mind, and I could see clearly what she was trying to show me. "I know you love your daughter and want to do whatever you can for her, but if you had a son, then your thinking would change. Sana might have to give up some of her rights, so that her brother could benefit."

I didn't want to agree with her, but I had seen this happen in other families, and it happened because our own mothers expected this from us. God had not made women any inferior in strength or wisdom; except for a small organ, we are both the same. Fatima could now see that the truth had finally found its way to me.

She continued, "I am not saying that we are bad mothers, but that we have ourselves enslaved our being into this cocoon of weakness. That's the reason we feel our lives were given to us in charity."

Fatima got up from her seat, and looked away from me. "It's not that my mother didn't love me. She would always tell me that she did love me, but in the end she would dote over my brother, and everything special was for him. I would get something if he didn't want it; that is why eleven years ago, when it came to choosing between us, not only my father but my mother left their weakling in the hands of this savage world."

I walked close to Fatima and hugged her. She turned towards me and held my hand tightly and said,

Promise me that you will tell these girls that you don't just love and care for them, but that they are precious, and that this life was given to them because they were worthy of life. It is a blessing from God, and no human can claim it as their charity. If they know that they are worthy, then they won't take their lives for granted, they won't let anyone hurt or harm their existence.

We are responsible for our lives. God has already provided us with the strength we need to protect ourselves and others. We do not have to wait for a savior; we are our own savior.

I looked at Fatima with tear-filled eyes; this simple girl who had suffered so much in life, still only thought of others. Fatima wiped my tears and said,

The time for crying is over; it is now time to live and enjoy God's bounty. The day we women are convinced that we too have the right to live, be happy and successful, without having guilt pangs that we are stretching the boundaries laid down by disillusioned women like us – only then will we be truly grateful to God for his blessing, called 'life'. It is time that every woman who turned this world into a 'MAN'S WORLD' should finally change it back to 'OUR WORLD', that's what God intended.

I knew there was so much more Fatima wanted to enlighten me with, but the crowd had finally subsided and we could see the officers returning to the van.

Fatima turned her back to me, and silently walked and sat in the van.

The senior officer came to me and handed me a legal paper, with details of Fatima's arrest and charges. The van started to roll down the hill. I kept staring at Fatima, who was no more looking at me, and within seconds even the police van was no longer visible. The street was getting empty; everyone had had enough for that day. The show was over, and no one wanted to wait for the curtain to fall.

I finally unplugged my feet from the spot where Fatima had left me, and I turned around to find my way back home.

The sun was just setting, the sky was a warm red, and clouds of dust were beginning to settle down. All the street stores were closing shop early today, there was so much in the air tonight that hearts were either left burdened or confused. My heart was very tired; my mind was slowly coming back to reality.

Amidst the dim lighting of the street diffused by the clouds of dust, I saw across the street a man sitting on the sidewalk. His head was hopelessly clasped between his knees and even though I couldn't see his face, I could recognize that figure – it was Sheraz.

Sheraz looked like a child who had lost every hope. I wanted to cross the street and sit by him, but I myself felt so helpless, and I had no words that could comfort him. I just wanted to fall apart, and crumble into dust; this all had been too much for me to handle.

I looked up into the evening sky, and my heart called, "Mom, please help me."

As I started to drag my feet forward, I saw a little girl, who was meagerly dressed; her face looked very dirty and sad. She walked straight up to Sheraz and tapped him on his head. Sheraz looked up. His face was flushed like the color of his heart, but he held the little girl's hand affectionately and asked what she needed.

The girl spoke very fast, but I could hear her from where I stood.

She said, "I'm very hungry, can you buy me some biscuits?" Sheraz smiled; he removed his handkerchief from his pocket and wiped her face clean. Then he held her hand and started to walk towards the tea stall. He bought her some milk and biscuits. I knew Sheraz's healing had begun. What I didn't hear was this: when he asked the little girl what her name was, she replied, "Sharmeen."

My heart was lighter and hope was beginning to show me its face again. There, about five hundred feet in front of me, I saw my daughter Sana, walking with another girl from the shelter. I knew they were looking for me and Fatima. Sana's eager eyes sighted me, and she snatched her hand from the other girl and began to run towards me.

I spontaneously and eagerly began to run towards her. When we met, Sana jumped into my arms, and asked, "Mom where were you? We have been looking for you for so long."

I hugged her tightly and began to kiss her all over her peachy face; I looked deeply into her honest eyes and said, "Do you know you are so precious?"

She giggled and began to kiss me all over my face and said, "Mom I know that."

Then she said something that stilled my heart, "Mom, you too are precious, do you know that?"

About the Author

Waheeda Soomro was born in Mumbai, India and moved to the USA in 1994. She comes from a family that was engulfed in an atmosphere of music and writing, her father being a very prominent composer and poet in India. UNSPOKEN is Soomro's first novel to be published. She has been an ardent story creator from the age of sixteen, and this year she has begun writing down and sharing all the stories that have haunted her thoughts for year.

All of Soomro's stories are based on women's social issues. She seeks to be a vigilante for their cause, using her pen instead of a sword.

She lives in the quiet suburbs of New York, with her husband and a daughter.

Acknowledgements

My most sincere thanks to my sister, artist Sayeeda Khan, for being the wind beneath my wings. It is her belief in me and my work that gave me the courage to come forward with this book. The cover illustration is a painting of hers, done about fifteen years ago, that never left my mind.

My thanks to Mirza Iqbal Ashraf, poet and philosopher, who has had many of his books published here. I am grateful to him for his moral support and encouragement.

My immense gratitude for my husband, Amjad Soomro, for his tireless technical support in publishing this book.

Lastly but not least, I would like to thank my editor, Shanti Fader Whitesides, for being so patient with me, as I took my first step in the field of writing. Beyond this world, my deepest thanks to God Almighty, for giving me the sensitivity to feel the pain of others, and the skill to write about it.

Made in the USA
Charleston, SC
01 June 2013